Planet Iggy

The Place Where Italian Greyhounds Talk

A book of short stories
by
Samantha Rose

Pigaloo Press
Perth, Australia

PLANET IGGY

ISBN: 978-0-6481594-0-7 (Paperback)
ISBN: 978-0-6481594-1-4 (Hardback)

Cover artwork by Dejana Louise
facebook.com/pg/DLouiseART/about/?ref=page_internal

Cover design by Mac Bros Book Stuff
Facebook.com/SabreBane/

Dedicated to my Mum Avice Stocken who never got to write her book, but always believed that animals could talk

Disclaimer

This book contains mild coarse language and is not suitable for children. It has been written for grown ups that have the imagination to envisage what their animals would say if they could talk.

All stories are fictitious and any resemblance to real life dogs or their owners is purely coincidental. After all, who would like to admit to their own dog smoking, drinking dog beer, and going to skimpies bars to watch beagles dancing with no collars on? You would get yourself locked up if you admitted that.

What more can I say except thank you for purchasing my book for which 10% of every book sold will be donated to the Italian Greyhound Club of Western Australia (IGCWA).

TABLE OF CONTENTS

CHAPTER ONE

How it all Began

I can't remember at what age I started talking to animals and imagining what they would say if they could talk back, I would like to tell you that it was when I was a small child but that would be a lie. I do believe it was at some point in my late twenties when I bought a rescue whippet bitch called 'Rema'.

Rema was a stunning blue whippet with a white stripe on her nose; four white paws and ears sticking out like the handlebars of a bicycle.

She would grumble if we ever told her off and would give out a sulky sigh that clearly demonstrated how pissed off she was. Rema would slowly and resentfully walk off to her bed while growling and giving a sideways glance, which translated as an act of rebellion and foul language.

"I swear she is talking to us." I would say to my husband who would reply that he swore that she was swearing at us and I reckon she probably was as well.

The talking animal situation escalated when we got our ginger cat Gordon who came into our lives as a nine-week-old kitten. His facial expressions and behaviours soon had me visualising him talking, swearing and having a social life.

I began writing stories about him and making him talk in my blog, and these very same stories assisted me in raising $3,000 to pay for his export and quarantine from London to Australia, but that is another story entirely.

In 2008 we moved to Australia and adopted a rescue kelpie dog called Rocky who quickly became firm friends with Gordon and still is to this very day.

Obviously, it wasn't long before Rocky started to talk and pretty soon other animals in the street began to voice their opinions and once they started, it was nigh on impossible to shut them up.

Our third and final pet was Brutus, a kelpie/ ridgeback. He came to us as a foster-dog in 2012 aged 12 weeks old and never left. Brutus is part of our furry family and enjoys his life with his two brothers Rocky and Gordon.

So how do you make animals talk? Everyone's relationship with their pet will vary, some just see them as pets, some see them as working animals, and some see them as family members equal to that of the human kind.

But one thing is apparent, and that is the closer the relationship between the pet and their owner, the more the owner will be able to 'read' their pet and vice versa. It does take a certain type of person to be able to talk to animals and understand them, and that is the message I try to get across to people.

All animals can talk, we just have to choose to listen to them, and that is a skill not everyone has.

This is a book of short stories about my dogs Brutus and Rocky and a group of Italian Greyhounds (AKA Iggies) plus a few other dogs. The stories are told from the animals' point of view, and they talk, sometimes swear, and have active social lives.

The inspiration for this book and the characters in it comes from some of the Italian Greyhounds that I know and have spent a huge amount of time with.

This book is what I would call a children's book for adults, and a sense of humour is required to enjoy it.

So read on, step into my magical world of talking animals, and after you have read this book, you may well see your pets in a whole new light.

But before you do anything else, grab yourself a cuppa and put your feet up, this is your private time, and you deserve it.

CHAPTER TWO

About the Italian Greyhound

In case you are interested, here is a bit of information on Italian Greyhounds, which I shall refer to as 'Iggies' in this book.

Italian Greyhounds are sight hounds. Their weight range is anything from 3.5kgs to 5kgs (for show dogs), but with pet dogs, obviously that can vary depending on how they are raised and how much they are fed. Their height is approximately 32-38cms, and the average lifespan for an Italian Greyhound is 13 years, but some have exceeded that.

Iggy Character

Iggies have great characters and make wonderful pets. They are good watchdogs and can do a powerful 'bup bup' bark to alert their owners to visitors, trees blowing in the wind and invisible monsters that frequent their garden.

If you don't know what a 'bup bup' bark is, then I suggest you find someone that owns an Iggy and go and knock on their door and listen to the bark because it does sound just like 'bup bup'.

Iggy Likes

Iggies love hanging out with their friends at Iggy play-dates, attending social gatherings where food is involved and generally being the centre of their owner's attention and universe. Remember that you can never love an Iggy too much and you can never spoil one too much either.

Iggy Dislikes

Iggies dislike the rain and may even melt if exposed to it. Cold weather requires a warm coat and make sure it is glamorous please because these little dogs have standards.

Dieting of any kind upsets them, and they will not hesitate to make their owners feel guilty for even mentioning the word 'diet'. Their ability to stare food from your plate and into their mouth is remarkable, and before you know it, you have shared half your meal with them.

They do not like being treated like a normal dog, they are far too special for that and they hate being ignored.

Pros of Italian Greyhound ownership

Iggies are a loyal, intelligent, loving, and kind breed of dog to own.

You get to go on Iggie play dates where you will meet some great like-minded people to discuss all things Iggy related, a bit like a mother and toddler group but for Italian Greyhounds.

Obsession is part of Italian Greyhound ownership, and you will start to spot unknown Iggies in the street and make a fool of yourself while trying to attract the attention of their owners to interrogate them about their dog.

Cons of Italian Greyhound ownership

You can't just stop at one, some people have two, and some people just collect them. Your entire world will revolve around your Iggy so trust me on that one.

CHAPTER THREE

Main Characters

I would like to introduce you to some of the main characters in my book, obviously this list is not exhaustive, but don't worry, I shall let you meet the others as they pop up in my head and make sure that you don't miss out.

Pippin Potter – Italian Greyhound (Bronte's brother)

Pippin is the head of the Italian Greyhound club, general organiser of everything and speaks with a BBC English accent. He is a quiet dog but is not afraid to be firm with the dogs in his group when he needs to be.

His home comforts are very important to him, and he has a tendency to burst into tears when he is tired or can't articulate what he is trying to say.

In his spare time, Pippin enjoys playing chess and climbing down women's sweaters, especially if they have large breasts.

Bronte Potter - Italian Greyhound (Pippin's sister)

Bronte loves fashion and is obsessed with her appearance and nice clothes. She is a popular dog among her peers and is known for her class, elegance, and sophistication.

She has a good heart, and if she believes in someone, then she stands by them and is a jolly good friend to have on your side.

A polar opposite to her brother Pippin, Bronte sometimes finds Pippin's sensible attitude challenging and enjoys teasing him.

In her spare time, Bronte attends fashion shows and does doggy Pilates in the garden.

Rocky – Australian Kelpie (My dog and Brutus's brother)

Rocky is an elderly disabled kelpie who doesn't particularly like other dogs because he was attacked in the past. He has become a part of the Iggy group and likes to hang out with them because they are small and of no threat to him.

Rocky is sensible, intelligent and has been to university where he obtained a degree in sheep herding and graduated with honours. He wears Harry Potter style spectacles and reads 'The Kelpie Times' which is a local newspaper just for kelpies.

He has an ability to peer at you disapprovingly over his glasses, just like your old school teacher probably did. (Let's face it, there is always one teacher that does that).

In his spare time, Rocky attends disabled sports classes where he is practising tennis ball games for dogs with bad hips.

Brutus - Ridgeback/Kelpie (my dog and Rocky's brother)

Brutus is a large, clumsy dog with a huge heart. He is dyslexic and has trouble learning things, which often makes him a target for bullies. He is your typical grubby teenage dog and often has poo stains on his bum, farts and belches a lot and looks like he needs a good bath.

Brutus is Pippin Potter's good friend, and although he really doesn't fit in with the 'Pointy Snout' club, Pippin fiercely defends him and has made him an honorary Iggy and protector of the group.

In his spare time, Brutus enjoys lure coursing where he is trying to master the art of turning corners instead of crashing through the barriers.

Madame Gigi - Italian Greyhound (Rocco's sister)

Madame Gigi is one of the older Iggies and the matriarch of the group.

Gigi wears designer clothes, oversized sunnies and she can turn heads anywhere she goes. She gives off an air of being famous and can shrivel you up just by looking at you. If you see any dogs shrivelled up on the pavement, chances are that Gigi is responsible by merely staring at them.

In her spare time, Gigi takes gentle walks in the evening and decorates old dog kennels for dogs less fortunate than herself.

Nica – Italian Greyhound (Zara's sister)

Nica is one of the smaller Iggies, and like Gigi, she is glamorous, sophisticated and keeps the younger dogs in order. She is tough, and you wouldn't want to mess with her, just ask the boxer Frugal McGuff who appears in this book later on, and he will vouch for that.

Nica is the Queen of broken legs as she has broken her own legs a couple of times and is now known as the 'Bionic Dog'. Being a sensitive dog, Nica can get herself so upset that she gets into more States than Australia. She can actually make herself vomit on command if she can't get her own way.

In her spare time Nica holds Italian classes for beginners, and on a Sunday she likes to dig the garden.

Zara – Italian Greyhound (Nica's little sister)

Zara is otherwise known as 'Zara Bobble-head' because she is clumsy, runs around until her internal batteries run out and tends to hit the walls and hurt herself. She wears a special crash helmet to protect her head as she has had a few head injuries while trying to negotiate obstacles.

Zara's favourite hobby is dodge ball, well it would be but she is far too fragile to play it so just pretends she does to impress her friends and look cool.

Vader the boxer (Brutus's friend)

Vader doesn't have many friends as 'non boxers' don't get him, but the friendship that he has with Brutus is quite special.

He talks in a slow voice, farts a lot and enjoys a bit of body slamming with other boxers. This sometimes results in flapping jowls, flicking of snot and a lot of growling. It may sound like a dogfight, but it isn't, because they soon forget what they were fighting about and as quickly as it started, they go back to playing again.

Rocco – Italian Greyhound (Madame Gigi's brother)

Rocco like many dogs has invisible friends that he enjoys fighting with when real friends are thin on the ground. He is prone to sudden displays of bad language and growling at nobody in particular, and if things are really bad, he will bite his own legs and make himself cry.

Some say that he has Tourette's and who knows if dogs can get that, but if you could hear Rocco having one of his verbal tantrums, you may be inclined to agree.

In his spare time, Rocco enjoys digging up plants and stealing his owner's underwear whenever he gets the chance.

Fat Harry – Italian Greyhound

Fat Harry as his name suggests, is fat or he prefers the term 'cuddly'.

Harry is a self-proclaimed foodie and a fully paid up member of his own 'Famine Club' which is a club for dogs claiming to be in a state of famine rather than the state of Western Australia.

In the past he has stolen food from BBQs and tables and has perfected the art of swallowing sandwiches whole and making his throat go 'sandwich shaped'.

In his spare time Harry attends a weekly slimming club where he has been caught smuggling in dog treats and selling them to fat Labradors in return for cash.

Dash - Italian Greyhound (Giovanni's brother)

Dash is another member the 'Famine Club' and can sneak into any kitchen and steal food with the skill of a 'Food-Ninja' (I have just made that word up, but I bet there is such a thing).

Both he and Fat Harry have become firm friends and regularly have 'Famine Meetings' which involves acquiring food that is not theirs and eating it quickly before it can be taken away from them.

In his spare time Dash likes to write stories about food and how to look hungry on a rainy day.

Giovanni – Italian Greyhound (Dash's brother)

Giovanni is known for his urination skills and is partial to peeing on dog's heads, something he finds absurdly funny.

He is a handsome dog that has made gorgeous babies in the past and still talks about the 'glory days' when he had his testicles. Giovanni is a regular on the social circuit and hangs around celebrity dogs trying to convince them that he is a male model.

In his spare time, Giovanni hangs out with famous dogs and studies photography.

Chewy – Tibetan Spaniel (honorary Iggy)

Chewy is a sensible and refined little dog and views himself as more superior than the others in the group. He doesn't like getting dirty or anything that messes his fur up and tells everyone that he is a distant cousin of Queen Elizabeth II.

In his spare time, Chewy runs his own deportment classes for dogs wishing to better themselves.

Georgina – Pug

Georgina is a small dog with a big dog attitude. Steal her food, and you could be in for a fight with Georgina on top of you biting the crap out of you until you relent and apologise. She does not conform to fashion, much preferring to create her own unique style. In her spare time, Georgina likes to do punk-ballet and bake dog biscuits.

Shelby – Italian Greyhound (Phoebe's brother)

Shelby is a fine looking specimen who was once admired for his testicles, which disappeared when the Testicle Fairy took them. Shelby is still resentful over this and regularly surfs the Internet for testicle replacements.

In his spare time, he runs a support group for neutered dogs and enjoys oil painting and humping his blankets.

Phoebe – Italian Greyhound (Shelby's sister)

Phoebe is a delicate dog with a tendency to believe what the other girls tell her.

One time she ate a wasp because Bronte

told her that it would be just like having Botox. Her snout swelled up, and she had to be rushed to the vet, so she never did that again.

Phoebe is kind and generous and has been known to give her last bone to dogs in need. In her spare time, Phoebe likes to hold dinner parties and listen to opera.

Eugeen the Angry Afghan

What can I say about Eugeen? He is a grumpy, handsome, black Afghan hound.

He is flamboyant, and he is fully aware that this attracts the girls. So with this in mind, he ramps it up for attention.

In his spare time Eugeen is a professional dancer and choreographer and he also plays the piano.

Kaya – Italian Greyhound

Kaya tends to hang around the big dogs instead of the Iggies, so we don't hear too much about him.

He is famous for his smile, and his lips have a habit of sticking to the top of his teeth, which gives him a lisp.

In his spare time, Kaya enjoys a game of chess, wearing multi coloured leg warmers and playing the harmonica.

These are just some of the characters, so keep an eye out for the new dogs that may pop up in each chapter.

CHAPTER FOUR

How I met Pippin Potter

I remember the day that I met Pippin Potter the Italian Greyhound and his friends and subsequently got drawn into the world of small dogs and pointy snouts. It was at a lure-coursing event, and I had brought my dog Brutus to enter him for a couple of runs. Aside from my friend Lucy and her dog Vader the boxer, we didn't know anyone at the venue.

Lure coursing is when a dog chases a mechanical lure down the track. It doesn't matter how fast they run or walk, as it is just good fun for them and a chance to catch up with their doggy mates and talk about their achievements

Brutus and I were walking around the field to warm up before the runs started when we noticed a group of Italian Greyhounds standing under a large gazebo.

"Hi there, my name is Nica, who are you?" smiled a pretty fawn Iggy who could not have been more than 3kgs when soaking wet.

Brutus looked around to see who she was talking to and realising that she was talking to him, he blushed.

"Hey, big dog! I am talking to you. Haven't seen you around these parts before." Nica held Brutus's gaze to encourage him to talk back.

"Piss off, this is our patch, and there is no room for big dogs like you," an aggressive voice seemingly came out of nowhere. Next to a table was a wire crate with a red fawn Iggy in it who looked absolutely furious at life in general. The door of the cage was open, but the Iggy inside refused to get out and was biting the bars of the crate to vent his anger.

"Rocco don't be such a meanie!" Nica snapped at him, "Ignore him; he has arguments with himself, swears a lot, and he hates everyone except for his invisible friends."

"Invisible friends?" Brutus looked puzzled.

Nica nodded vigorously, "Oh yes all dogs have their own invisible friends, but they usually only come out when toys or beds have exploded and then we blame our invisible friends so that our parents don't tell us off.

"Sometimes it works, and they believe us, but even when it doesn't, it is still nice to have invisible friends to run things by and all that stuff." Nica pointed in the direction of Rocco who was having a heated argument with himself and chewing his hind legs for moving without his permission.

"Now then, you didn't tell me your name?" Nica persisted and wagged her tail, "And by the way, the grumble-bum in the cage is Rocco - my brother."

Realising that he would have to answer Nica, Brutus took a deep breath, "Brutus, the name is Brutus, and this is my first time here, and I don't really have any friends except for Vader." He could feel his cheeks burning, and as he had no experience with girls, he found himself awkward and clumsy.

Nica stared at him and watched him kick the soil with his paws and fumble around looking for somewhere to put himself and her heart positively melted at his embarrassment. It was at that moment that she decided that if Brutus didn't have many friends, then she would take him under her wing and introduce him to the Italian Greyhound club and the world of small dogs and big personalities.

"Rocco, wouldn't you like to say something to Brutus?" Nica barked at him.

"Bollocks!" Rocco snapped and started to wash his anus.

Rolling her eyes, Nica nodded towards the other Iggies that were having an animated discussion about clothes. "This is our lot, they can get a bit raucous, but in the main, they are a good bunch, come on I shall introduce you."

Some of the Iggies were talking in high-pitched Italian accents as though they had inhaled large volumes of helium. There was one white and blue Iggie that stood out from the crowd, he was speaking to the group in a noticeably English accent (I call it 'BBC English').

He was holding several mobile phones, a leather diary and one of those computer mini tablet things that are all the rage and he seemed to be holding court to the entire group and looked pretty important for such a little dog.

"Ermmm I am not really sure about this..." Brutus stuttered and looked around for Vader the boxer, but before he could finish, Nica was announcing his arrival.

"Excuse me you lot, I have a new friend for you, his name is Brutus!" and without warning and in one swift movement, Nica jumped on to Brutus's back and shouted over everyone in order to be heard.

They all stopped talking and stared at Brutus with Nica perched on top of him like a mountain goat. A black female Iggy with a greying muzzle squealed "Oh my god, it's a giant! It's a giant! Call the zoo, call the police, this dog could kill us all with one bite!"

Then with a flurry of dramatics, the black dog fainted but kept one eye open to see if she was getting attention, which of course she wasn't as the others had ignored her and all stepped over her to get a better look at Brutus.

"What is it, a horse?" One of the Iggies asked as he walked around Brutus and formed what is known as a 'man triangle'.

"Don't be silly Carlos, he can't be a horse as he doesn't have hooves, I am Deejay by the way, and that is my brother Carlos," one of the Iggies raised a paw to Brutus to greet him, "You are not an elephant are you?"

You must have heard of the 'man triangle' and that is where guys are shown something like a car or a large power tool, and they all walk around it in a triangle shape to suss it out. They never do suss it out of course but if doing that makes them feel better then who are we to argue

"Well, whatever he is I think we need to tie him up and attack him just in case." One of the Iggies insisted as several others agreed, their high-pitched voices becoming louder to make themselves sound aggressive. Their bravery would have been quite admirable had they not been hiding behind a table or each other.

Brutus's bottom lip had started to quiver, which it always does when he is about to cry. Feeling overwhelmed and frightened, he tried to make himself look smaller by crouching down to his belly and burying his face between his front paws causing Nica to fall off on to the ground with a thud.

"Ouch! Now look what you have done, you have scared him!" Nica growled impatiently.

"I am not an elephant, I am Brutus, and my Mum said that I am a good boy." He mumbled to reassure himself in between trying to catch his breath from crying.

"Hi Vader, who is this giant and do we need to attack him?" a female red and white Iggy asked Vader the boxer who had come to see what Brutus had been up to.

"That's my friend Brutus, isn't he marvellous? He does all the same stuff as me, and he is dead clever as he can jump on top of cars, he is just like a boxer dog except that he isn't." Vader said proudly to the group of Iggies who were hanging on to his every word.

The white and blue Iggy that had been holding court to the others held up a paw to silence his gang, and after a few minutes he barked, "Well, he looks OK to me, and if Vader says he is OK then he must be."

"The name is Pippin, Pippin Potter and I am the head of this bunch, pleased to meet you." Pippin smiled warmly at Brutus and then gave a paws-up sign to the rest of the group to try and settle them down.

"This is my sister Bronte," he pointed at the pretty red and white girl that had approached Vader earlier. "And I believe you have met Rocco and his invisible friends already?" Pippin gestured at Rocco to behave himself in his crate and to stop pulling threatening faces.

The Iggies looked up at Pippin for reassurance and then at each other to gauge the general consensus, "Make a false move, and you are dead!" Rocco sneered from his cage and curled his lip.

"Yeah, dead!" sneered an overweight Iggy who was making hissing noises at Brutus.

Bronte stared at Brutus who was still shaking. Any dog as big as Brutus that was so frightened of dogs as small as Italian Greyhounds, surely deserved sympathy. He could, of course, be useful, they didn't have a bodyguard of their own and Brutus would certainly look the part of a protection dog.

"Here, come with me - I can show you around." Bronte smiled and held out her paw. With his legs still shaking, he walked behind her while trying not to admire her little bottom, which wriggled as she walked.

"I've got my eye on you!" Rocco slunk out of his cage and growled and repeated to nobody in particular, "I've got my eye on him." He continued to point his paws at Brutus and then back to his own eyes to emphasise the fact that 'he had his eye on him'.

Pippin remained where he was and watched Bronte and Nica lead Brutus forward and in turn, accept him into their group. Secretly he felt proud of his team because they had dealt with it so well and proving that it's not all about judging someone on their appearance. Because for all Brutus looked big and tough, Pippin had quickly realised that he didn't seem to have a bad bone in his body and the biggest thing about him, appeared to be his heart, oh and his ears because let's face it, his ears are enormous.

The Iggies started to follow Nica, Bronte, and Brutus. Slowly gaining their confidence and trust in the big dog, Brutus had been made to feel so welcome that it was as though he had known them all his life and vice versa.

"Brutus, we are all going to have so much fun together!" Bronte beamed.

"Brutus, would you mind if I stand on you for a few minutes?" Rocco asked him in an unusually polite voice. Now out of his crate, he had totally forgotten about keeping an eye on him and was trying to win the big dog over.

"Erm, well, no that is fine, you can stand on me..." Brutus stuttered, not having any idea as to why Rocco wanted to stand on him.

"Thanks, you are such a sport," Rocco said appreciatively and leapt up on to Brutus's back and quickly inhaled the remains of his Mum's hot dog from her plate.

It was at that point the Iggies knew that Brutus would fit in with their little gang just perfectly.

"I think he is going to do OK with us, don't you?" Nica asked Pippin who had been watching the whole thing.

Pippin looked thoughtful and opened a page in his diary titled 'Iggy Members List', grabbing his pencil he added a name at the bottom 'Brutus' and by the breed section he hesitated somewhat and wondered what to write. After a few minutes, he wrote, 'Big Fella'.

"Yes, I think he will fit in with our lot jolly well." He nodded.

From that day forward, Brutus became one of the Iggies, and because at that time he was a puppy himself, he did indeed become just like an Italian Greyhound in terms of mannerisms and behaviour and until this very day, still believes that he is not a 30kg Ridgeback/Kelpie, but in fact a 5kg Italian Greyhound.

And that my friends, is where the story starts.

CHAPTER FIVE

Pet Cafes – The new black

When it comes to our pets, there certainly seems to be a market to cater for those of us that like to spoil our animals. Even when a recession is affecting businesses everywhere, you will always find animals lovers willing to spend their hard earned cash on toys, clothes, anything pet related and in more recent times it has been pet cafes.

We have a couple of pet cafes in Perth that are specifically aimed for your pet, of course you are invited, but your dog (or cat) is the primary and most important guest and believe me when I say that there are no shortcuts in terms of how nice the set up is inside these establishments.

In this chapter, I am going to talk about one of the favourite 'hangouts' of the Iggy gang, and that is the Furbaby Cafe, which opened in Perth in December in 2014.

I have just picked out one of the pet cafes in Perth, as I have been to this one myself and this establishment have approved this chapter for publication

Furbaby Cafe

Furbaby Cafe is one of the cool places for dogs and their owners to hang out in Perth. Some have described it as the animal version of a star studded eatery where all the famous people hang out, others have said that their dogs refuse to dine anywhere else and how 'Furbaby is the new black'.

Either way, I have been there a few times myself and have found it a pretty impressive place so it seems only fair that this cafe should have its own chapter in my book. So if you don't live in Perth, Australia, you can at least get a glimpse into Perth's smartest cafe for 'cool' dogs.

Furbaby sells a wide selection of dog clothes, treats, collars, leashes, toys to name but a few. The food menu has delights such as doggy lasagne, biscuits; even custom made birthday cakes, all of which is made from healthy dog-friendly ingredients.

They have two sections in the cafe, one is the public area, and the other is the 'VID' section (Very Important Dog) where you can hire out a private, securely fenced off and sheltered part of the cafe for doggy birthday parties, club meetings and gatherings for a very reasonable fee.

As far as the scenery goes, I cannot even begin to describe how nice it is and how the staff made a dog cafe so comfortable that the humans would want to frequent it often, but they did, and now it is one of the most sought after places in Perth to host your dog's party.

Italian Greyhounds and Furbaby Cafe

So what is so special about this cafe and its relevance to Italian Greyhounds? Well, I shall tell you, but you have to promise not to get too jealous because you are a human and will never get to enjoy it from an Iggy's point of view.

Italian Greyhounds are fragile; they have what I describe as legs that snap like carrots. Although they can give as good as they get when it comes to chasing and doing 'zoomies' around the park, they are also prone to injuries and a larger dog playing boisterously could have disastrous consequences for an Iggy.

Having a nice safe place for the Iggies to play off leash and socialise while their owners can enjoy a coffee or a bite to eat is a godsend, and Furbaby Cafe provides this.

The Iggy gang plan their events carefully, and some will turn up with new outfits to show off to their mates. Other Iggies see it as an opportunity to get food that they wouldn't normally be allowed to have. There is no such thing as a diet when you are at a Furbaby function for either humans or their pets because the food is quite frankly delicious. (I had the tastiest cooked breakfast there once)

The public part of the cafe is spacious with beautifully arranged seating and tables. There is an Elephant fountain in the corner for dogs to drink from. I am not sure about the dogs, but I would quite like to drink from it myself although I probably wouldn't do that, as it would get people talking.

The Furbaby reception and shop are a dog's delight because it sells clothes, toys and doggy cakes and treats to take away. There is a grooming salon on site so that dogs can get bathed, clipped and spruced up while their owners enjoy a coffee.

It is common to see dogs in the shop pestering their owners to buy them a toy and resistance is pointless because rarely do people leave the cafe empty handed and I know that from personal experience.

"Mum, can I have this, please? Pippin Potter has toys from here, why can't I?" Brutus demanded when we were at someone's birthday party one time. I did try and say no to him but what can you say when your dog grabs a honking hedgehog dressed in camouflage gear and starts throwing it around the shop to make it honk?

I ended up buying it of course and Brutus was so pleased with his toy, that he declared it to be the best day ever as he happily carried his hedgehog back to the car.

Another time I left with a leather look cap for dogs in the largest size possible after I had an assistant search for one big enough to go around Brutus's enormous head. My husband still hasn't forgiven me for that one.

Whenever there is an Iggy event at Furbaby, the group always meet up in the shop (by the toys of course). This is where you can witness a mass of tails wagging and pointy snouts, as Italian Greyhounds greet their friends as though they haven't seen each other in years; when it was probably only the day before.

If you can imagine them all air-kissing and saying 'Hello darling!' admiring whoever has the best dress, wearing Italian designer sunglasses and speaking in fake Italian accents. That's not counting Pippin Potter as he speaks in a BBC English accent and sounds like Winston Churchill about to announce the war.

The greetings go on for about 20 minutes until their VID private party commences. Then their leashes are removed, and the dogs can run around, pee on the plants provided and patiently wait for their owners to order food.

A birthday cake will have been ordered, and it is always as good if not better than any human cake I have ever seen and looks tasty enough for humans to eat. When the Furbaby staff and the owners sing 'Happy Birthday' the Iggies always cheer whoever is celebrating their birthday.

Once everyone has eaten, at least one person will venture to the shop and come back with gifts for their dogs, and whatever has been purchased will be proudly shown to everyone else.

Dogs saying things like 'Oh look what my Mum bought me!' followed by 'Does my bum look big in this?' or 'Oh my god, I am not wearing that!' or 'Do you like my squeaky toy?'

If you are on the outside listening in, you can hear laughter, barking, chatting and the sounds of cutlery clanking on plates. But most of all, what you do hear just makes you want to be in there yourself joining in with the fun.

The end of an event

When the party comes to a close, the Iggies are always exhausted and ready to go home; usually one or two of them have to be carried out because they are so tired. At least one of them will be complaining that they will never eat anything again because they are so stuffed. Some of them have to undo their pants because their bellies are so full of food; mind you I am sure that has happened to us all at times.

It can take at least 15 minutes to leave Furbaby Cafe because the staff make a fuss of the dogs so saying goodbye can take a while as you can imagine. Dogs are kissed, Iggies admired and of course, no day is complete without the purchase of a toy as I mentioned earlier.

I will say that the next time I go, I am determined that I won't buy Brutus anything but you all know what it's like, it takes a heart of stone to tell your dog that he can't have the squeaky toy that he has stolen off the shelf let alone make him give it up. If they had clothes in his size, I would be buying him a leather look waistcoat, but then I reckon even the Iggies would disown him if I did that or certainly my husband would.

The journey home

The journey home is a quiet one and involves snoring Iggies with full bellies, dreaming of their afternoon at Perth's smartest pet cafe with promises to call each other to make it happen again soon. Which it always does because there never seems to be too long between events and each event brings new excitement, recognition of a familiar friendly place and a catch up amongst friends.

Dog cafes, they are not just for dogs, but also enjoyed by their humans and are a nice place for your dogs to hang out.

Furbaby, it is the magic behind that wall, the place where it all happens. It is where the latest doggy gossip can be heard, where designer clothes can be purchased, where dogs drink out of an elephant fountain and have their own plants to pee on.

It is where your dogs get waited on hand and foot and finally, it is a place where if it's 'not in' then it's 'out'.

Pay it a visit some time.

The End

CHAPTER SIX

Pippin the brave

Friends as we know, come in all shapes and sizes and it is no different when it comes to animals, and we would be foolish to think otherwise.

Pippin Potter has a wide circle of friends and could be described as a 'Social Butterfly'. He attends most of the Iggy gatherings and is always organising something whether it be a meeting or a session of bitey-face games around his house. His friends are all the same size as him except for Brutus, and he is a very unlikely friend for an Italian Greyhound.

From the very first day that they met, Pippin looked out for Brutus by making sure that Rocco didn't scare him with his outbursts and that the girls didn't frighten him off with their naughtiness.

Pippin Potter and Brutus became firm friends, and as their friendship grew from strength to strength, nothing could split them up, and if any other dogs ridiculed Brutus, they were met with a sharp tongued reprimand from Pippin and the other Iggies in the group.

On occasions, friendships can be tested, and a real show of strength is when you have to defend your friend against something that you are scared of yourself. Because to not defend them is not an option, so if that means standing alone and making your voice loud enough to be heard then so be it.

Sometimes that means being a good friend can be hard, as Pippin and Brutus both came to learn at different points during their friendship.

The Dog Show

One day Pippin was at a dog show, and Brutus had plans to come to cheer him on. Pippin had arrived much earlier in order to be groomed and prepared, and Brutus had planned to get there a couple of hours later. It was to be the first time that Brutus had entered the world of show dogs and one that he wouldn't forget in a hurry either.

Brutus always feels that he needs to announce his arrival, I don't know why but he does, and there is no changing him of that habit. He does this at the vet and expects the nurses to all greet him as though he is the only dog in the surgery and sometimes it gets quite embarrassing.

On arrival at the show grounds, an excited Brutus looked around to see if he could spot the Iggies. He had to go past some dogs that were either being groomed, chatting to each other, or lying in their crates reading glamorous doggy magazines.

A German Shepherd dog (GSD) was busy gossiping with her friends, "Of course she didn't know that she had anal glands and wondered why her bottom was leaking!" laughed the GSD as her friends shrieked in exaggerated horror at whoever they were talking about.

"Well, I said to her that the closest she would come to a show dog is watching it on TV!' another GSD said loudly, 'I mean, who does she think she is?" then stopping mid sentence the dog noticed Brutus standing there wagging his tail to get their attention.

"Hello there, the name is Brutus, I am here with Pippin Potter, do you know him? He is my friend." Brutus said to the group of GSDs.

A strained silence came over them as the two GSDs tried to stifle their laughter while one of the dogs actually circled Brutus and looked at him as though he could have been a dinosaur.

"And what breed of dog are you? Because you certainly are not a pedigree." The dog sneered at him.

Brutus stared at the ground and pretended that he was interested in the stones. Feeling his heart pounding, he didn't trust himself to respond so he said nothing and tried his hardest not to cry.

"Excuse me, but I asked you a question. You are clearly not a pedigree and certainly not a show dog so what kind of dog are you apart from a hideously ugly one?"

"My Mum said I look very handsome," Brutus whispered.

"My Mum said I look very handsome", the GSD repeated as she tried to mimic his voice, which made two other GSDs plus a couple of poodles laugh raucously.

Brutus bit his lip and fought back the tears. He was used to being loved and adored by his circle of friends, and this kind of hostility was new to him.

He didn't always grasp situations or understand things, but Brutus knew that these dogs were not being nice to him and he didn't have the social skills to deal with it. He was truly on his own. If he could just find his Iggy friends, he knew that he would be OK, but Pippin and the rest of the gang were nowhere to be seen.

"Handsome? More like a joke I reckon," a French poodle scorned which made all the other dogs laugh and pretty soon there was quite a gathering around the large gentle brown dog who was so overwhelmed and upset that he had started to cry.

"My Mum loves me, and she said I am nice, and that is all that matters." Brutus kept wiping his eyes and snotty snout.

"Hey where did you get those ears, do you pick up radar?" a perfectly manicured Yorkie giggled and encouraged her friends to join in.

Too terrified to move, Brutus just stood there and cried, he wanted Pippin but most of all he wanted his Mum.

Pippin Potter to the rescue

"Bronte, have you seen Brutus? He said that he would meet me here half an hour ago." Pippin asked his sister who was standing on a grooming table being prepared for her next class.

"Sorry Pip, haven't seen him, why is there a problem?"

Pippin didn't answer, but he had a feeling about this, and it wasn't a good one either.

Deciding to go and look for himself, Pippin trotted across the grounds looking to see if he could spot his big friend. Sighting a crowd of dogs of various breeds by the entrance, Pippin wondered what was going on, but as he got nearer, he froze and felt physically sick at what he saw.

Brutus was crouched down on the floor on his belly trying to cover his ears with his paws, with loud heartbreaking sobs that could be heard for quite some distance as the group of dogs all stood around him poking him and laughing at him.

On closer inspection, Pippin saw that Brutus had urinated on himself and a Maltese terrier was announcing it to anyone that would listen and everyone that wouldn't.

Pippin was terrified. He would be no match for those dogs and was outnumbered and so for the first time ever, the normally well-organised and assertive Pippin, did not have a clue what to do or how to react. He could walk away of course because Brutus hadn't seen him, or he could go and get his Mum, but that really would not help either, because this was dog-talk and only dogs could sort it out.

For what seemed like ages, Pippin watched Brutus try to hide his face in his front paws as he howled for his Mum and his favourite Tony Abbott doll that he often used to comfort himself, while the group of dogs continued to draw attention to the fact that poor Brutus had wet himself.

Pippin recalled how Brutus allowed him to stand on his back at Furbaby Cafe so that he could steal food from the plates. He remembered how Brutus had let the other Iggies snatch bacon from his mouth and he remembered how Brutus would let him hide underneath him when he needed 'time-out' at parties. That was when Pippin realised that loyalty and bravery are not measured in kilos or size, and he had to do something to help his friend.

"Does your Mum know that you have wet yourself Mr Big Ears?" a French mastiff bitch sneered at him.

"I am a good boy, I am a good boy, my Mum said I am a good boy, Brutus is a good boy, Brutus is a good boy!" Brutus kept chanting aloud while trying to cover his ears.

"Brutus is a good boy! Oh my god did you hear that?" the mastiff said to the rest of the dogs in the group.

Then seemingly out of nowhere, Pippin Potter came running at considerable speed and barged his way through the group nearly knocking some of the smaller dogs over.

"Pippin, is that you?" Brutus said in a wobbly voice and slowly started to stand up.

"Oh hi Pippin, how's it going? Have you met this hideous looking thing?" a GSD sniggered to Pippin.

Pippin stared coldly at the GSD and said nothing.

"What's the matter Pip?" the GSD asked him, "You don't know him do you?"

"HE is MY friend, and his name is Brutus. There is nothing ugly about him, in fact, I think he is the best looking dog in this show!" Pippin snarled.

The group of dogs fell silent; the GSD stared at Pippin, "Don't tell me that is your friend? He is not even a pedigree!"

"Well, check you out Mrs Clicky Hips, I don't actually think you should be in the show either, but here you are in all of your...." Pippin tried to think of what else to say "In all your ugliness and nastiness!"

"As for you, well you have no face so may I suggest that you go and find it?" Pippin said pointedly to the French Mastiff.

"And YOU, you look like a curtain pelmet on wheels." he spat at the Maltese terrier.

One by one, Pippin dished out scathing insults to every single dog in that group, and he said it in such a way that if they didn't have a complex before the show, they certainly had one now.

"Come on old chap, our tent is over there, and there is a crate with your name on it," Pippin said gently to Brutus, "Don't hang around with this lot, you might catch something."

Leaving the group of dogs looking like someone had murdered their mother and served her with dog chow, Pippin guided Brutus back to the Iggy group.

"You were so brave Pippin, I was petrified, were you not scared?" Brutus whimpered.

"No, I wasn't scared, I could have handled them all at once and made them cry." Pippin lied.

Staring at his friend in admiration, Brutus felt as though his heart would burst with pride. Anything was possible when you were friends with Pippin Potter, and nothing else mattered when you were with him either.

"Pippin?" Brutus whispered to Pippin.

"Yes, Brutus?"

"I have wet myself, I didn't mean to though." Brutus sniffed and looked down at the urine dripping off his legs and staining his fur.

Pippin laughed, "Oh that's OK old chap, we shall just tell everyone that it was Giovanni, after all, you are nobody until Giovanni has peed on you." Giovanni has a habit of urinating on other dogs and has made a sport out of it.

Back at the Iggy area

Brutus was soon settled in his crate, and Pippin had told them all that Giovanni had peed on Brutus and had done such a good job of convincing everyone that even Giovanni himself believed that he had done it.

"I must say I don't remember pissing on Brutus, but then again, I probably did. Sorry, Brutus, it was rather rude of me." Giovanni said apologetically.

Brutus smiled, "No worries Giovanni, I kind of feel part of the gang now you have done that."

"You are part of the gang and always have been." Giovanni patted Brutus affectionately on his leg.

It was those words that meant so much to Brutus that he was already starting to feel better.

You can't polish a turd (or can you?)

Pippin had rounded up all the Iggies and had told them about what had happened to Brutus (except the peeing part), and this was not very well received at all. Luciano was threatening to shred his own blanket as he was so angry and begged for everyone to hold him back or he might get aggressive.

The word had spread around Pippin's friends, and they were not happy and wanted revenge. A gang of pugs wearing leather jackets were demanding justice for Brutus, and the best way to get justice is not to get mad but to get even.

"Brutus, can you come here please?" Pippin asked him. They were planning something, but the question was would it be effective?

One hour later

Bronte and one of the pugs in a leather jacket had gone to get some of the dogs that had bullied Brutus. "But why are we here Bronte, you know our tent is by the entrance?" a GSD said impatiently.

"There is a new rare breed of dog here, he is rumoured to be worth $10,000 at least, and he has been imported from Egypt," Bronte said firmly as the group of dogs stared at her wide-eyed in disbelief.

The GSDs and the mastiff raised their eyebrows at such a claim but as curiosity got the better of them; they nodded and replied: "OK, let's see what you've got."

The Iggies and pugs stood in front of one of the crates, obscuring much of the view. Pippin nodded to the group to give instruction, and as they moved to the side of the crate, there stood Brutus stacked beautifully like a show dog. His coat had been glossed over to make him look like polished pine and beside him was a ribbon that had been placed on the crate giving the impression that he had won it.

"Oh my god it's THAT dog!" the mastiff gasped.

"But how?" the GSD said shaking her head.

A couple of Maltese Terriers moved closer to check Brutus out.

"This my friends is what they call a 'Frutus Hound and it is from the Upper Regions of the North of the River Nile." Bronte gushed, feeling quite proud of the name she had invented.

"A Frutus Hound?" Giovanni whispered to Bronte who nodded vigorously.

"Don't touch what you can't afford and trust me champ, you can't afford this one." Giovanni sneered as they tried to get closer.

"Erm, sorry Brutus, we didn't realise, is there anything we can do to make it up to you?" the GSD stuttered.

"I don't think so do you?" Bronte butted in.

"There is just one more thing." Giovanni barked, and without warning, he cocked his leg and pissed all over the GSD's legs causing the other dogs in the group to laugh.

"Oh look, you've peed yourself." Giovanni said calmly and then turned around and walked back to the back of the Iggy gazebo taking Brutus and the Iggies with him, leaving two of the pugs in leather jackets making cut-throat gestures while growling "So long Clicky Hips!"

Back at Pippin's House

After the show, Brutus went back with Pippin to his house to discuss what had happened. They sat side by side in the garden while soaking up the sun and just enjoying each other's company.

"Pippin, I don't know how to thank you for today, you were so brave, and I don't know what I would have done without you," Brutus said to him.

"You would do the same for me I know you would," Pippin replied.

Sometimes when it comes to defending your friends you have to step out of your comfort zone, and Brutus realised that after today, Pippin was right, he would totally do the same for him.

"Thank you for being my friend today Pippin." Brutus nudged him with his huge boofy head and nearly knocked him over.

Pippin wagged his tail and playfully poked Brutus in his ribs.

Then as the two dogs stretched out in the sun, Pippin asked Brutus, "I say old chap; you don't mind if I use you as a pillow do you?"

"Not at all Pippin, that's what friends are for." Brutus smiled and then adjusted his body so that Pippin could rest his head on him. And that was precisely where they remained until Brutus went home.

As I said, friends come in all shapes and sizes.

The End

CHAPTER SEVEN

You've Gotta a Friend in Me

Bronte had been a bit secretive lately and had taken to hiding stuff from Pippin and the girls. It was Madame Gigi that had initially raised concerns, which at first Pippin had dismissed because he thought that girls were born to have secrets. In fact, Rocco told him that girls had secrets buried in their hearts as well as their collars.

But Madame Gigi is a savvy little dog who knows things, some say that she is a walking wealth of knowledge, others say that Gigi can even predict storms and disasters but that, of course, could just be a rumour. Either way, Gigi had picked up on Bronte being secretive, and she was going to make it her mission to find out what was going on.

At Pippin and Bronte's House

"Are you off out again?" Pippin sighed as Bronte packed her little purple rucksack and slung it over her back.

"Yes Pippin; and I don't have time to talk about this now as I am in a hurry, so don't wait up!" Bronte snapped.

Before Pippin could say another word she had left, slamming the door behind her and leaving

Pippin wondering what on earth was going on and thinking surely she couldn't have a boyfriend?

Pippin was just about to get back to working on his diary when he heard a beeping of a mobile phone. Looking around to see where his phone was, he realised that it was, in fact, Bronte's phone and she had left it behind. Biting his lip, he wondered if he should read the message and then quickly reprimanded himself for being nosey.

"But isn't that why I have a long nose so that I can be nosey and can keep an eye on the safety of the group, after all, they all depend on me," he told himself and then stared at Bronte's phone for a few minutes as it kept flashing to alert him of the unread message. Knowing that Bronte didn't lock her phone because she was too lazy to unlock it, Pippin told himself that it wouldn't really be snooping because if she were that concerned about anyone reading her messages, then she would lock her phone for sure.

He nervously opened the message and read it, 'See u layter, carnt wayt 2 cee yoow - lluv B' was all it said.

Scratching his ears, Pippin's first thought was what kind of idiot had written that? It must be some secret dog code for 'When you are on heat next will you have my puppies' or something but whatever it said, he could barely make head nor tail of it and who the hell was 'B'? It couldn't be anyone from the Iggy club, as they were all highly intellectual and could not only excel in obedience but could spell the word backwards.

It was a mystery, and whoever it was, Bronte had gone out to meet them and was hiding it from Pippin and the group. Picking up one of his mobile phones, he dialled Madame Gigi's number.

"Hi Gigi it's me, Pippin, yes I am very well thank you, listen I don't suppose you have a few minutes do you?"

The Next Day

Some of the girls were all around Nica's house holding a 'collar, clothes and leash party' where they all get to look at collar and leash catalogues and order stuff if their parents let them. Most of the parents do let them because if they don't, then beds explode all over the garden, so it is generally easier to allow them to use their credit cards purely for a quiet life.

Nica, Gigi, Bronte, and Zara were chatting about the latest designer collars and which jackets would go with the diamond collars. Bronte kept checking her phone and was looking fretful when she saw that there were no messages for her. "Bronte, is everything OK my friend?" Gigi asked her.

"Oh yes, fine thanks," Bronte growled back.

"Expecting a call?" Gigi smiled with an expression that told Bronte that there was no point in lying because Gigi was 'The Queen' of knowing when people were lying and had an admirable ability to wrangle the truth out of anyone. (My Mum used to be like that and knew when any of us kids were lying without us even opening our mouths)

"Nope, just checking the weather," she said sharply, "And I think it is going to be distinctly chilly," Bronte added while admiring her freshly painted nails.

"Well, as long as you know you can talk to me - about anything," Gigi said in a quiet voice as her huge eyes bore into Bronte making her blush and feel guilty for whatever it was that she was hiding.

Just as Gigi was about to get up and go to the kitchen, Bronte's phone rang causing her to startle. "Hello, yes fine, give me 30 mins and I will be there, no, that is OK I promised you didn't I?" Bronte tried to whisper down the phone while holding her paw to cover her mouth to muffle the conversation.

Except that it didn't work because Gigi had heard everything and if looks could melt ice, Bronte would have turned in to a puddle.

"Be careful Bronte, there are many dogs out there that would take advantage of a nice dog like you, and you could end up in the pound if you are found on the streets and remember that there are no designer collars in the dog pound," Gigi said sharply and quickly turned on her heels leaving Bronte alone.

"Sorry Pippin, I tried," Gigi said to Pippin afterwards leaving Pip wondering what to do next.

They were all worried for Bronte because it is quite common for female dogs to be attracted to bad dogs that roam the streets and work on corrupting the bitches to make them do naughty things like raid trash cans and poo in the middle of the street with no thought for anyone that might tread in it.

A large male boxer in the area called Frugal McGuff was rumoured to have at least four bitches in his group, and he had trained all of them to steal bones from the butcher and treats from the pet shop.

One of them is a beautiful show whippet that got pregnant to Frugal and ended up producing a litter of puppies that had snub noses, and her owners cried for weeks after that. Especially as they had paid to have her mated with another whippet and hadn't realised that Frugal the boxer had got in there first. Those puppies took a lot of explaining to the new owners as they were expecting whippets with a snout as sharp as a biro pen.

So you can see why everyone was worried for Bronte and now Gigi was convinced that Bronte had fallen in with bad company and could start to get naughty or worse still, mix with Frugal McGuff who obviously has a thing for girls with pointy snouts.

A Week Later at Frugal McGuff's House

Frugal McGuff was lying on his bed with a couple of kelpie bitches that were scratching his fleas for him. Cans of empty dog food lay scattered on the floor, a DVD about dog training was being watched in the other room by a chunky black Labrador with the name 'Anne' engraved on a rusty ID badge attached to her tatty pink leather collar.

Outside Frugal's house, Pippin waited behind the hedge. Nica and Gigi gestured for Pippin to stay put as he always stuttered when his nerves got the better of him, besides they felt that Gigi with her 'resting bitch face' could freeze the testicles off the devil himself.

With a 'take-no-shit' kind of look, Gigi nodded to Nica, "Let's do this!" and between them managed to hammer the crap out of Frugal McGuff's door causing all the dogs inside to 'bark the bark' of their people.

Without looking up and only showing mild interest, Frugal yelled to Anne the Labrador "That will be the door then, go and answer it, there's a good girl."

Anne looked boot-faced at the demand because she was always being asked to get the door and believed that it was because she wasn't as slim and as pretty as the other dogs. She had tried to diet, but the words 'diet' and 'Labradors' do not really go together the way 'Pies' and 'Labradors' do.

Anne heaved herself up to open the door, and as she did, she was met with Gigi and Nica who barged past her and went straight in to Frugal's living room. "Charming!" Anne the Labrador sulked as she looked at Nica and Gigi's slender figures while wondering if they had to starve themselves to look like that.

"Hello there, ladies, to what do I owe this pleasure?" Frugal McGuff spoke in his boxer voice (boxers all talk with fat tongues and have slow voices, or they do in my stories anyway).

"We are not here for your company McGuff, where is she?" Gigi stood right up to Frugal's face, followed by Nica. Both dogs were positively bristling with anger at the thought that Bronte might be there.

"How bloody rude of you!" Anne shook her head at Gigi who ignored her.

Anne the Labrador was feeling so insecure about the two Iggies and their slinky figures, that she had reached up on to the table and had stolen a bread roll. Scoffing it in one go, she almost choked in the process as she desperately tried to swallow it without anybody noticing.

Frugal cocked his head to one side "Bronte? The red and white Iggy with the nice bum?" He looked thoughtful as he tried to think who Bronte was and after a few seconds of visualisation, he gave a lecherous look, "She isn't here, but if you fancy organising it so that she could be, I am sure I could find a space for her in my basket."

"She isn't here? Frugal if you are lying to me I swear to god I shall have your testicles served on a plate!" Gigi snarled at him flashing her white canines making herself look almost demonic. The kelpies giggled in the corner, and one of them even snorted as she laughed.

"And you can shut up as well!" Gigi growled at the snorting kelpie who quickly hid under the pillow and started chewing on a tennis ball.

"No really, she isn't here ladies so if you would excuse me I have more pressing matters to attend to," Frugal said impatiently and grabbed the remote control and pointedly changed the channel as if to dismiss Gigi and Nica. "Anne, show our visitors the door please."

Gigi actually believed him because she knew from experience that boxer dogs are terrible liars and have even been known to take the blame for other dog's mistakes. If Frugal said he hadn't seen Bronte, then he was more than likely to be telling the truth.

Anne reluctantly got up and waddled to the door, with a deadpan expression on her face she growled sulkily "Goodbye then." and as Nica and Gigi walked out, the door slammed behind them.

"Who is this Bronte?" one of the kelpies asked Frugal.

Frugal sniffed, "Don't know but I wouldn't mind finding out." And with that, he sat back down and stared blankly at the TV while stuffing bone shaped treats in his mouth and farting at the same time.

Back Outside

Nica and Gigi went back to Pippin who was hiding behind the hedge. "What's happened? You were ages in there, did you get Bronte?" Pippin spoke quickly as he was nervous.

Gigi shook her head "No, she wasn't at Frugal's house Pippin and to be honest I don't actually know where she is."

"Sorry Pippin, whatever Bronte is up to, she is not doing it with Frugal McGuff," Nica replied sounding disheartened.

"Oh dear oh dear." Pippin thought to himself, this really was no good at all.

At Pippin's House

Pippin was back at home and Bronte wasn't. He hadn't got a clue where she was and she hadn't even returned home for her tea and Pip felt terribly worried about her. He was just about to go to bed when he heard the door open and Bronte creep in with a rucksack on her back; she looked exhausted and went straight to her bed.

"Where have you been Bronte? We were so worried, we even went to Frugal McGuff's house to see if you were there!" Pippin blurted out and then unable to hold back anymore, he burst into tears as he often did if he got frustrated or tired.

"Frugal McGuff! Frugal McGuff! You thought I was with Frugal McGuff!" Bronte shrieked and then started laughing, "Pippin how could you think I was with Frugal McGuff?"

"Well, who were you with?" Pippin demanded in between sobs.

Bronte's face went blank, "I was busy and you don't need to know who I was with but it was certainly not Frugal McGuff, my goodness he has mated with half the stray dogs around here." Then without saying another word she went straight to her bed.

"Bronte?" Pippin whispered to her.

"I am tired Pippin, leave it please." she said from under her blankets and Pippin had no choice but to do just that.

Pippin the Detective

As Gigi and Nica couldn't find anything out, Pippin had decided to try and find out for himself what was going on with Bronte and had made his mind up to follow her the next time she went out on her own.

Dressed up in a different collar, a tatty raincoat, black gloves and a bowler hat, Pippin figured that if he dressed like the spies did in old English films then nobody would recognise him and he could be 'incognito'. Rocco had tried to tell him that 'Incognito' was an Island off Furbaby Cafe but thank goodness Pippin didn't believe him.

"See you later Pippin!" Bronte shouted and grabbed her precious rucksack that neither Pippin nor anyone else was allowed to touch. Slamming the door behind her, Bronte disappeared past the living room window.

Pippin crept out and followed her, hiding behind cars and trees so Bronte couldn't see him. Occasionally she looked around if she heard a noise or something but other than that she was focused and hell bent on getting to her destination. While Pippin was hell bent on finding out exactly where that was.

After following Bronte for several kilometres Pippin realised that he was at the local park where the Iggy play dates were often held. What on earth was going on? Finding a large tree to hide behind, Pippin sat down to get his breath and at the same time, keep an eye on Bronte who was nervously standing by a bench and hopping from paw to paw.

Her mobile phone beeped with a text message, Pippin watched her smile as she read it and quickly text back a response. Whatever she was up to, he was about to find out.

A huge canine figure appeared in the distance, sheepishly walking up to Bronte while wagging his tail. At first Pippin had to strain his eyes for a few minutes but then he had to rub his eyes to prove that he wasn't dreaming. There standing next to Bronte was Brutus gripping a brown satchel as though his life depended on it.

"You made it! I was worried you wouldn't come, we don't have much time you know." Bronte said sounding relieved that he had actually turned up.

"I was scared and I nearly got lost," Brutus replied in a shaky voice.

Pippin gasped at what he saw. Brutus was his best friend but there is no way in the Planet of Iggy he would ever be suited to match up with Bronte. Just as he was about to barge in and demand to know what was going on, curiosity got the better of him and he remained behind his tree to observe them a bit longer.

"Today we are going to learn how to read using colour pictures and drawings.

"I know you struggle with words Brutus but I have heard that you can tell a whole story from just a couple of pictures," Bronte said as she carefully laid out some brightly coloured pictures of the Christmas Nativity plus some coloured crayons and paper for Brutus use.

"I don't understand?" Brutus panicked as she spread everything out on the bench.

Bronte patted him on the back "Don't worry, let's take it slow and I will have you ready to read your part at the Christmas Nativity so don't fret."

"I am so ashamed Bronte, everyone would laugh at me if they knew." Brutus looked embarrassed.

"Ashamed? Nothing to be ashamed of my friend, being dyslexic just means you have to learn things a different way.

"And there is nothing wrong in being different, that is what makes the world go 'round" Bronte handed him a red crayon to do some more pictures.

Pippin quietly crept away leaving the big dog and the little dog sitting next to each other chatting. He had seen all that he needed to see and knew exactly what he had to do when he got back home to make everything right.

Back at Home

When he got home the first thing that Pippin did was call Gigi, "Hi Gigi, it's me Pippin, I know what is up with Bronte".

"What is it, is she OK?" Gigi replied.

"Yes, she is fine, she has just been helping out a friend so no need to worry, and everything is just great."

"Thank goodness for that Pippin, I was quite worried there for a moment." And you could just hear the relief in Gigi's voice.

In bed that night

Bronte and Pippin were curled up in their beds ready to go to sleep. Pippin could see Bronte's shadow on her bed tightly curled up in a ball with her pointy snout tucked neatly against her bottom to keep warm.

"Bronte?" Pippin asked her.

"Not now Pippin, please don't ask me where I have been, it's been a long day and I am tired." Bronte sighed.

"Sorry I accused you of seeing Frugal McGuff, I know you would never go near him and I am sorry for hassling you and pestering you. I have asked Gigi and Nica to not ask you again either."

Bronte lifted her head up and looked at him "What brought this on?"

Pippin puffed his cheeks out to think of a suitable reply, "Oh I have just realised what a fabulous sister I have and that I should never have doubted you."

Bronte laughed, "Can I have that in writing, that I am fabulous I mean?"

Both dogs settled down to go to sleep, occasionally burying their heads into the blankets.

"Oh Pippin?" Bronte whispered.

"Yes, Bronte?"

"Frugal McGuff! Really?" Bronte giggled.

Then all you could hear were the muffled snorts of laughter from Pippin and Bronte at the mention of good old Frugal McGuff.

At Brutus's House

Brutus lay in his bed with a blanket over his head and under the blanket he was holding a torch trying to read some notes and pictures that Bronte had written for him, titled 'The Christmas Nativity - Iggy Style'. You could just see Brutus's mouth trying to read it and work out what it all meant.

He had just a couple of weeks to get ready to take his part in the Christmas Nativity. Would he be ready for it? Who knows, but with Bronte helping him, he would no doubt do just fine.

The End

CHAPTER EIGHT

The Christmas Nativity

Every year at Christmas time, the Iggies put on an event of some sort, which involves drunken debauchery and lots of high jinx. But this year Pippin Potter wanted the Iggy club to do something a bit more respectable and decided to do the Christmas Nativity Iggy style.

Pippin hoped that the dogs would learn many valuable life lessons from doing the Christmas Nativity or even just one lesson would be nice.

"But what can we possibly learn?" Fat Harry asked Pippin one day.

"I don't know, but I am sure there must be something." He replied. Pippin had been looking forward to this event for ages and had dreams of well-behaved, well-trained Iggies with no rudeness or swearing or anything. Yes, yes, I know, a dog can dream can't he?

It wasn't going to be like your traditional Christmas Nativity story as Pippin had 'tweaked' it and adapted it to suit the Iggy club. That was OK though, as the Christmas spirit was there plus peace and goodwill to all dogs with all the warm and fuzzy feelings to go with it.

The big day

The story had been written, the actors had been cast and lots of rehearsing had been done. It was now the night of the event, which was to be held at a secret venue.

Bouncers had been hired in the form of Teddy a French mastiff and Sultan a staffie, both dressed up in leather jackets, with white shirts and bow ties and looking extremely dashing. One could be forgiven for thinking that Iggies do not need bouncers but Pippin didn't want to take any chances and the two big dogs looked every inch the protectors (and splitter up of squabbles) of the tiny dogs inside the building.

As with any production, there was plenty of excitement behind the scenes with sounds of barking, yelping and a lot of swearing which was not very festive but Rocco has always said that he was born with a few rude words in his mouth and to take him or leave him.

Brutus, Vader and Fat Harry were playing the three wise men and had all been given tablecloths or sheets from their owner's houses with bathrobe belts to tie around their waists to keep them in place.

Chewy, the Tibetan spaniel, was playing the baby Jesus, and he was already tucked up in his crib wearing a blue romper suit that he had picked out himself. This was after Vader had told him that the real baby Jesus wore it in biblical times. He was quite happy about his part because Chewy, like many dogs, was thrilled to be given the opportunity to lie in a crib and have to do very little.

Brutus was jealous of this and would have given his last bone to sleep in that crib, never mind the fact that he couldn't fit in it. It took some placating from Pippin to tell him that as well as being an overall 'Good Boy' he had the best part as a wise man and that the real Jesus would be so proud of him if he knew.

Nica and Shelby were playing the Virgin Mary and Joseph. Nica thought that she looked pretty cool in her sheet and had decorated it with glitter and Christmas baubles just to brighten it up. Shelby had tried to persuade Pippin that the real Joseph wore tight leather pants and a black satin shirt. He was pissed off when Pippin didn't believe him and made him wear a sheet like everyone else.

Georgina, the pug, had been cast as the guiding star and was suspended from the ceiling dressed in a shiny gold star costume. With a mischievous grin on her face, she rocked back and forth from the rope, with her hind legs kicking out trying to swing far enough to touch the huge Christmas tree in the corner.

"Georgina, must you show QUITE so much enthusiasm? I don't think stars are meant to swing like that!" Pippin shouted up at her.

"Oh star of wonder, star so bright, Rocco set my knickers alight!" Georgina sang as she built up momentum on her rope and carried on swinging.

"Did she just say her knickers were on fire?" Shelby's sister Phoebe asked Carlos.

Carlos snorted and said yes, she did say her knickers were on fire and how rude was that?

"Right everyone, lights, camera, action!" Rocco barked through his megaphone.

The audience waited in anticipation as dogs and owners alike sat proudly in their chairs, each convinced that their pet would be the best.

"My Fat Harry is a wise man, I am so proud of him," Fat Harry's Mum Carla said to an old lady sitting on the chair next to her. The lady was noisily sucking on some chewy mints and spraying some rather overpowering lavender perfume around her to disguise the smell of mothballs and urine.

"That's nice dear, would you like one?" The old lady offered Carla a mint, which had melted in its wrapper.

"How kind but no thank you; oh look here come the wise men!" Carla clapped excitedly as things started to happen on stage.

The curtain at the side of the stage was moving and Fat Harry came skidding across the stage on his bum as Rocco shoved him out with so much force that he nearly knocked Chewy out of his crib.

"What did you do that for?" Fat Harry shouted at Rocco who flipped him the bird and poked his tongue out.

Fat Harry stood up and cleared his throat, "I am one of the wise men and I am checking to see where baby Jesus is. Although I am bloody useless at map reading so he could be anywhere by now."

"Oh my god, that is not part of the Christmas nativity!" Carla said to Pippin's Mum, Janice who was sitting a couple of seats away from her.

"No it most certainly isn't." Janice agreed, well nothing surprised her with this lot and it certainly shouldn't surprise anyone else either.

"I think Pippin is letting them do their own thing this year." Janice shrugged, "but it could all end in tears of course and probably Pippin's."

Brutus and Vader had started shuffling along the stage. Taking his place next to Fat Harry, Vader adjusted his belt and looked in the audience for his Mum. Spotting her he started to wave and nearly whacked Shelby in the face at the same time. Brutus followed him and took his place and checked that he could see me in the audience as well.

"That's my Mum over there; look everyone it's my Mum! Love you Mum!" Brutus pointed to me and waved while I did a discreet wave back with one hand and covered my face with the other while the audience laughed.

"How far do we have to go?" Fat Harry asked Brutus.

Ignoring him, Brutus glanced up at Georgina who was dangling down kicking out her legs, momentarily forgetting that he was in the play with an audience, "Oh look Harry, it's Georgina swinging from the roof, hi Georgina, how are ya doing?" Brutus waved to her as the audience erupted with laughter.

Pippin covered up his eyes and wondered if these Hollywood directors had these kinds of problems with their cast, probably not.

"This is hopeless." Pippin mouthed to Rocco who was smoking a catnip cigarette and trying to throw darts at a badly drawn dartboard on the wall.

Vader poked Brutus in the ribs "How far till we get to the Inn to give Mary and Joseph their presents?"

Holding a GPS, Brutus tapped it a few times with his paws, "I am not sure, it says that the address is not found, but the nearest address is the pet shop, will that do?"

"Let me look, I am sure you haven't put in the right postcode, have you tried Bethlehem?" Vader tried to snatch the GPS from Brutus who twisted around to stop him taking it.

Looking confused and tapping the GPS again with his paws, Brutus tilted his head and asked how to spell 'Bethlehem'.

"Just put in the pet shop and we will see what happens." Vader agreed as Brutus tried to work out how to spell 'Pet Shop'.

The dogs were re-writing the script and there was nothing Pippin could do about it except maybe cry quietly into his blanket and wonder where it all went wrong.

Rocco being the director had tried to make sure that things went smoothly, but ended up fighting with himself in the corner and calling himself a bastard.

"We shall continue to walk until we find Mary, Joseph and baby Jesus." Fat Harry commanded as Brutus and Vader dragged their feet to follow him with Brutus occasionally demanding to know 'if they were there yet as he was tired and could he go for a poo?'

Anyway, the three (not so) wise men arrived at the inn where they were met by Nica and Shelby playing the part of Mary and Joseph. Chewy lay swaddled up in a puppy blanket in the crib as the baby Jesus, full of his own hair and importance.

"So what have you brought me, it had better be good and none of that cheap shit from down the road?" Chewy snapped, he threw himself into the character and decided that perhaps baby Jesus would have been given more gifts had his parents been more assertive.

"You are so ungrateful," Fat Harry tutted, "Don't you all think that he is being ungrateful?"

Nica was filing her nails and looking bored with it all while Shelby was playing games on his mobile that he had sneaked in under his robe.

Fat Harry marched forward holding a bone and said to Mary and Joseph "I bring you a bone from my home".

A puzzled Nica stopped filing her nails and glared at Shelby "Isn't it meant to be gold, frankincense and myrrh?"

Shaking his head Shelby replied, "Not sure, I thought it was a squeaky toy myself or perhaps a beef chuck bone. Never heard of myrrh, what is that?"

Rolling her eyes, Nica made a mental note to teach these dogs about the real Christmas nativity.

"Quick, you are next!" hissed Rocco to Vader and gave him the thumbs up.

Vader took his place with his squeaky pink pig. "I bring you my finest toy which is my pig, but don't chew it as my Mum bought it for me."

"Thanks." Chewy tried to take the pig but Vader held on to it and wouldn't let him.

"You are meant to give it to me as my gift," Chewy said impatiently.

"But that's my pig and it's my favourite." Vader protested and a small tug-of-war ensued over the toy and it nearly ended up in a fight until Nica coughed loudly and distracted them leaving Vader looking upset with his tongue hanging out like a Christmas ham.

Placing his head in his paws and pretending that he was somewhere else, Pippin Potter wished the floor could swallow him up. These dogs were making it up as they went along, could things get any worse? Oh god yes they could because now it was Brutus's turn as the third wise man.

Brutus is not very good at reading and he has dyslexia. As you know Bronte had been teaching him to read by making stories out of pictures as you can tell a thousand words from a picture. For the Christmas Nativity Bronte had done some drawings on a small piece of paper that nobody knew about except for her and Brutus.

"Your turn Brutus, you are on!" Rocco signalled to him.

Brutus looked up and he could see the faces of the audience, he was sure that they were laughing at him. Unable to speak or do anything, he was completely frozen with fear and had completely lost his nerve.

I looked at him feeling quite sick for my big dog, secretly praying that he would regain his nerve and be able to remember his lines. The dog owners were all on the edge of their chairs wondering just what Brutus would do or say next.

"Oh god, he can't remember his lines." thought Nica as she stood over the baby Jesus's crib which contained Chewy who was trying to chew his bum through his romper suit.

"What's happening?" Chewy asked Nica.

"Shhhh! We are waiting on Brutus, he has stage fright." Nica whispered.

A painful silence hit the audience; a group of ridgebacks sat in their chairs and held their breath. Eugeen the Afghan hound (AKA the angry Afghan) was so nervous that he was smoking cigars while Millie the Border collie covered her eyes with her paws and only took occasional glances to see what was happening.

Brutus looked as though he was going to burst into tears. With his bottom lip quivering, he scanned the audience for anyone familiar to him.

Brutus moved towards the baby Jesus's crib with his precious Tony Abbott doll and a folded piece of scrap paper that Bronte had given him earlier. On it were a few very simple but brightly coloured drawings and nothing else. Fat Harry and Vader watched Brutus who was busy trying to unfold the piece of paper so that he could see it.

Clearing his throat he looked at the first drawing and saw a cartoon of some budgie smugglers, the second drawing was of a baby boy wearing a romper suit and the third drawing was of a Christmas tree with presents on it and a large paw behind it.

"Bloody hell, how is that going to make any sense?" Fat Harry thought.

However, it didn't need to make any sense to Harry or anyone else for that matter. It only needed to make sense to Brutus if only he would open it up and look at it. But instead he scrunched it up into a ball without even realising what he was doing.

"I have come to give my…" Brutus stuttered and then farted - something he does when he gets nervous.

"Jesus Christ!" Fat Harry wrinkled his nose and wrapped his robe around his snout while poor Nica pretended that she couldn't smell it and just held her breath.

"Did someone say Jesus, that will be me then!" Chewy piped up and stuck his head out of the crib.

"I think he is talking about an earlier model," Shelby smirked.

"Come on Brutus, you can do it!" Georgina cried as she swung from the ceiling.

All eyes were on Brutus who could only focus on the eyes of every dog and human in the audience while imagining the bristling disapproval of Rocco from the side of the stage.

"Brutus, look at me, look at me!" Bronte thought, secretly willing him to ignore everyone but her. "You can do it Brutus," Bronte said calmly as he caught her gaze and frantically looked for an escape.

"I want my Mum," Brutus said to nobody in particular.

"Oh dear, he wants his Mum, I can be his Mum." Lily, the Iggy from QLD, said to some of the other QLD Iggies that had made the trip down just to see the Christmas Nativity.

Gigi butted in, "You will have to fight me first because I would also like to be his Mum. Let's just say that he brings out my maternal side."

The dogs all continued to watch Brutus, his long legs were shaking so much that it was a wonder that they were able to support him. With his sheet wrapped around him, he wore a huge pair of fluorescent green sandals (Dash had insisted that they wore them in biblical times and Brutus believed him); Brutus stared at Bronte in the hope that she would know what to do.

Bronte smiled and nodded towards the piece of paper in Brutus's paw to encourage him to open it out to look at the pictures.

With sweaty paws, Brutus straightened out the piece of paper and looked at the drawings on it. After an embarrassingly painful and long silence, he remembered what he had to say and he said with a deep voice, "I present my favourite Tony Abbott doll to the baby Jesus," and then added "But please don't chew it as I would like that back, and my Mum said that I am a good boy." he finished.

It would have taken a hard person to not see the humour in what Brutus had just said and a boring one to not find it funny.

"Priceless!" Eugeen wiped his eyes as the rest of the audience clapped and laughed with Brutus and not at him.

"That's my boy!" Bronte said to herself and gave him the thumbs up signal (or paws up).

Rocco was furious as the dogs were changing the scripts to suit themselves. He told himself to 'Piss off' in the mirror and head butted his own head and then had to apologise to himself.

"Here comes the donkey!" cried Vader, forgetting that wasn't meant to be his line, but he said it so enthusiastically that the audience cheered and clapped for the donkey which was being played by Cesar the greyhound.

"Hi everyone, the name is Cesar, pleased to meet you." He nodded to everyone while one of his greyhound mates in the audience waved his collar in support.

"Excuse me, can we finish the show please, this is totally meant to be about me so can we please get on with it!" Chewy barked from his crib.

"Don't mind me, I shall just take this." Brutus snatched his Tony Abbott doll back.

"Actually if you don't mind I shall have this bone back." Fat Harry tugged the bone away from Chewy.

"I shall have my pig back as well," Vader added leaving an angry Chewy with no gifts.

"Excuse me, what do you think you are doing?" Chewy demanded, but by now the other dogs had taken their place to finish the show and Pippin was already lined up to do his speech.

"I say you can't just take stuff away from the baby Jesus! You will all be sorry for this, this is blasphemy I tell you!" Chewy leapt out of his crib to where everyone else was standing.

"You need to remember who I am, young man!" Chewy curled his lip at Vader and Brutus, "Stealing from the baby Jesus, whatever next?"

Nica had to remind Chewy that he wasn't really the baby Jesus and this was just a Christmas Nativity play but Chewy was already talking about lawyers to get his gifts back.

Fearing that there would be a huge row over the whole thing, Pippin decided to hurry things along and 'wrap things up' as they say in show business.

Speaking quickly Pippin addressed the audience and as he had forgotten the piece of paper with his well-rehearsed speech on it, he had to totally wing it.

"And so Mary and Joseph had their baby in the barn, the wise men came and delivered gifts to the baby Jesus and then took them back.

"Then everyone learned the art of being helpful and kind and lived happily ever after," Pippin spoke without taking a breath before anything else could go wrong.

The audience stood up and cheered, barked, clapped and yelped so loudly that the door dogs Teddy and Sultan thought there had been a fight and had barged in ready for action.

Shelby, Nica, Brutus, Vader, Fat Harry, Cesar and Chewy all took a bow as everyone clapped and stomped their feet and they wouldn't rest until Pippin came to the front of the stage where he was lifted on to Brutus's shoulders so that everyone could see him.

"Where is Georgina?" Nica asked Shelby.

"Oh she was hanging around up in the air last time I saw her." Shelby pointed up to the ceiling.

And so the clapping continued, they clapped for the actors, they clapped because they were all friends, they clapped for Brutus for being brave but most of all they clapped for their club leader Pippin Potter.

"So beautiful, I am so proud of my boy." Janice Potter wiped a tear from her eye.

"That is my brother, look at him, isn't he marvellous!" Bronte waved at Pippin.

"And he is our friend as well." a very proud Dash (Giovanni's brother) declared and all the Iggies nodded vigorously in agreement.

As the dogs lined up to sing the closing song for the Nativity, Madame Gigi took her place at the piano. "Is everyone ready for the final song?" Gigi said in a dramatic voice that she saves for special occasions.

They were ready, they were more than ready.

'Bark the kennels all dogs sing
Glory to the new-born king'
'Give us food and give us toys
Our Mums say we're all good boys'

'We didn't mean to dig the garden
Belch in your face and not say pardon'
'Bark the kennels all dogs groan
We deserve some juicy bones'
'We're all good dogs for our Mums
Who wipe our faces and dirty bums'

Teddy and Sultan stood inside to watch the closing of the show. They were silenced by the high-pitched voices of the Iggies, little dogs and the deep voices of Brutus and Vader.

"Teddy are you crying?" Sultan laughed at his brother and handed him a handkerchief.

"It's my allergies that's all." Teddy sniffed and then blew his nose noisily into Sultan's handkerchief before handing it back to him. There is nothing like the spirit of Christmas to get everyone all emotional and even security dogs can cry you know.

That's a wrap! (And Harry I don't mean a chicken wrap either!)

The show had finished, the venue was now empty and the dogs were all set to go home. Pippin was outside doing a head count as they all got on to the mini bus.

"Has anyone seen Georgina?" Pippin asked Nica who said that she hadn't seen her for some time. Pippin ran back inside to see where she was and unable to find her, he announced that Georgina was missing.

Rocco blushed and buried his head in his dog magazine and lit another cigarette to distract from his guilty face.

"Help, I am up here!" a little voice could be heard.

"Where on earth is that coming from, is that Georgina?" Madame Gigi looked around to see who it was.

"Excuse me, I am up here! This is not funny, get me down right now!" Sounds of distant shouting, growling and barking could be heard.

"What on earth is going on, Georgina what are you still doing up there?" Pippin stood on a chair so he could get a better look.

"I am stuck, Rocco hoisted me up high and tied me to the water pipe," Georgina growled. Still dressed as the guiding star, she had indeed been tied to a large water pipe that ran across the ceiling and had been there all that time.

"Rocco! I thought it was meant to be peace, goodwill and good behaviour to all dogs?" Pippin glared at him waiting for an answer.

And Rocco's answer to that involved his favourite word 'Bollocks'.

Back at Team Potter's House

After dropping Teddy and Sultan off at their home, the Iggies finally arrived back at Team Potter's house totally exhausted. Those that took part in the play were still in costume including Georgina who for some reason now had her star outfit on inside out.

Brutus, Vader and Fat Harry were wearing their robes, Brutus's had poo stains on the back and Fat Harry looked heavily pregnant as he had stuffed an entire bag of dog treats under his robe for later.

Pippin stood up to give his traditional Christmas speech which was usually about how the year went and who had achieved what. He generally tried to leave any wrongdoings out of it, as sometimes in life we all need to be told how marvellous we are.

"So what have you all learned this Christmas?" Pippin asked them all.

"That Georgina makes a good star." Rocco snorted.

"That Rocco is naughty." Georgina jabbed Rocco in his ribs.

"That I am not as generous with my toys as I thought." Vader looked at his squeaky pink pig.

"That I am not a brave dog and sometimes and I just want my Mum." Brutus blushed.

The other dogs had gone quiet. They knew that it was a huge thing for Brutus to get on stage today and even though he can't read properly, he made up the words from the notes that Bronte had given him. Not just ordinary notes either; these were pictures and drawings to help Brutus to remember.

They also realised just how far Bronte had gone to help her special friend and aside from Pippin, none of them had any idea that she had done this for him.

One by one, the dogs all dug deep and recalled how each of their friends had done something no matter how small, to help the others and once they started with the stories, they carried on chatting while Pippin just sat and listened with an immense feeling of pride for his little group.

"I would actually like to thank Rocco," Georgina said unexpectedly as the room fell silent and the dogs stopped talking.

"Why do you want to thank me for?" Rocco looked shocked.

"You may have pulled me up and tied me to the ceiling but for the first time in my life, not only was I a star but I was taller than all of you," Georgina said to him.

Everyone stared at Rocco as he hung his head down, "Sorry Georgina, I didn't mean to do that to you."

She smiled at him and wagged her tail, "That's OK, I'll bite your bum later!"

"If you can reach it that is!" Rocco laughed.

"Are you saying I am small?" Georgina pretended to raise her paws to smack Rocco and did a few cheeky boxing moves.

Rocco stared at the small dog with the big personality, "Small? You are many things Georgina, but small is not one of them."

"What have you learned today Pippin?" Bronte asked her brother.

Taking a deep breath Pippin replied, "I have learned that you can't plan everything but if you work hard you will get there in the end, with a bit of swearing of course." Pippin winked at Rocco.

"Right you lot, does anyone have anything left to say or can we get on with having our bones and toys?" Pippin asked them.

"Yes, I have." Brutus stepped forward. "Thank you for being my friends, it means a lot to me, Merry Christmas everyone." Brutus coughed after his speech and tried to hide his embarrassment by pretending to wash his bum.

"No problem my friend, no problem," Pippin stood up, "Merry Christmas everyone, now these bones are not going to eat themselves so let's tuck in."

The End

CHAPTER NINE

Pippins Guilty Secret

We as humans all have a guilty secret of some description, something that we don't like to be reminded of that could embarrass us, and our dogs are no different.

Pippin Potter had his own guilty secret, which he would have preferred to have kept hidden from the other members of the group. But like most things in life, these things have a habit of getting out and when they do, they are remembered forever and used in evidence against you and I know this from personal experience.

One evening Pippin was getting ready to go out and had been taking an unusually long time to get changed. He seemed to be in a hurry and as he went towards the garden door, Bronte looked at him and frowned, trying to think what was different about him. "You look a bit padded out Pippin, have you put on weight?"

Pippin put his head down and replied that no he hadn't put on weight; he was just wearing thick trousers as it was cold and a huge oversized raincoat to keep the bad weather out.

"But it is 34 degrees outside, how on earth can you think that is cold?" Bronte giggled and went back to reading her book.

"I always feel the cold more than normal Iggies, anyway I am off to the vet to see about enrolling in the doggy slimming club," Pippin said quickly to try to end the conversation.

Picking up his keys, Pippin said that he would see Bronte later but as he walked out of the door, some sequins fell from the inside of his coat. This of course attracted Bronte's attention and with the sequins was a business card that had 'The Dog Club' with a Fremantle address on it.

"Pippin! You have dropped something!" Bronte shouted after him but it was too late, he was gone.

Bronte checked the card and noted the address on it, she knew where that was as obedience was held there some days, but why did Pippin say that he was going to the vets for slimming club when he had just denied that he was putting on weight?

"I shall follow him." Bronte thought, but she couldn't go alone so she called the only friends she knew that were game enough to escort her and offer her protection as well. "Brutus, I need your help and bring Vader with you," Bronte said to him and like all good mates, Brutus quickly managed to get to Bronte's house with Vader the boxer to find out what was going on.

"What's up Bronte?" Brutus asked her when he arrived at the house.

"And whatever it is, does it involve food?" Vader added as festoons of drool dribbled out of his mouth.

"Wait and all will be revealed," Bronte said mysteriously and told them to get in the car. But what Bronte didn't realise was that after tonight she would never be able to look Pippin in the eyes again, at least not without having hysterics.

The Dog Club

Pippin had pulled it off and had successfully managed to fool Bronte and make his way to the Dog Club without her following him, or so he thought.

"Do you think they suspect anything?" Pippin asked Shelby.

"Not a chance" Shelby laughed, "By the way, do my balls look big in this?"

Pippin looked at Shelby; he was wearing tight white satin pants, flared at the bottoms with golden studs down the side and a matching top. With genitals of substantial size, Shelby's boy parts actually entered the room before he did, causing the bitches to ask him for his number and whether they could take a selfie with his testicles.

"They do look quite big, can you make them look... well, less big?" Pippin suggested enviously. Dear old Pippin, like Brutus he was not blessed in the genital department so it was only understandable that he was jealous but saying that

Shelby's 'boy parts' were comparable to Mother Nature giving him the best portion and saving the tiny bits for the rest of the Iggies (and Brutus).

"Do I look OK?" Pippin said self-consciously and then stood to the side and sucked his non-existent belly in to see if he had a 'pant bulge' that he could display to the boy dogs (Pippin loves boys). Wearing pale blue satin flared pants with gold studs down the side and a matching tight satin top, Pippin looked pretty awesome himself. But there was no more time to discuss one's appearance and genitals because names were being called and things appeared to be kicking off.

A chunky self-important looking beagle with a firm bottom stood by the main hall holding a clipboard and a biro pen to mark names off as everyone arrived. Chewing gum with his mouth open, he gave an air of insolence as he ticked each dog off his list.

"Hold on, hold on, don't just barge in; if your name isn't on the list then you can't come in!" snapped the beagle to a couple of French poodles. They were not happy about being reprimanded by the beagle and started to argue with him in a French accent.

"No point in talking double Dutch my friend, I can't understand you." The beagle growled and waved dismissively with his paw.

"It wasn't double Dutch actually, it was French." One of the poodles said with an insulted look on his face; it had taken him years to perfect that French accent. Telling them that they had to behave themselves or he would kick them out, the beagle turned his back on the poodles and went to assist a basset hound that had gotten wedged between two chairs.

Two chunky Staffordshire bull terriers were trying to dance together but ended up farting with each step and making each other giggle.

"Are you all ready?" The beagle barked through a small megaphone, "Take your places everyone!"

Eugeen the Angry Afghan sat at the piano ready to play. Wearing a pair of gold-rimmed spectacles at the end of his long snout, he ran his fluffy paws against the music sheet in readiness.

"Ready?" The beagle asked Eugeen who gave the thumbs up to signal that he was (ready).

"Let's go!" The beagle shouted as Eugeen started to play.

With a firm nod of his head and a flick of his long black ears, Eugeen dramatically moved his paws up and down the piano causing everyone else to say stuff like 'Ooh, isn't he good, I never knew he was that good' and some of the older dogs were actually asking if Eugeen had an album out.

You've Been Rumbled!

"I can't see, I can't see anything, can you lift me up at the window?" Bronte asked Brutus and Vader.

"I need to fart, does anyone mind if I fart?" Vader looked at Bronte for approval.

"Why do you ask, you normally just do it anyway?" Bronte wrinkled her nose, "Now please can you give me a leg up?"

"Get off my jowls!" Vader growled as Bronte jumped on to Vader and Brutus to get a leg up to see what was going on through the window.

"Can you see anything?" Brutus demanded.

"Not really, Oh my god it is Shelby!" Bronte jumped and almost pierced a hole through Vader's cheeks with her nails.

"Shelby! What is he doing in there?" Brutus whispered to Vader, "I bet he has brought his testicles with him, what a show-off!"

"Well, he can hardly leave them behind can he?" Bronte hissed at Brutus before looking back in the window.

"Oh my god it is Pippin and you will never guess what he is wearing?" She gasped.

"What are they wearing Bronte, tell us?" Brutus nudged her.

"See for yourself but you must promise not to laugh, you promise?"

"We promise." Brutus and Vader said solemnly but what Bronte didn't see was the fact that their paws were crossed behind their back, which in doggy terms negated the whole deal.

Jumping down to let the boys reach up and see for themselves, Bronte could not believe what she had seen and more to the point, how she was going to stop Brutus and Vader spreading it around the group like a bushfire.

"What a bunch of girls, what are they doing - Oh my god!" Vader choked on his tongue.

Brutus who was standing next to him stood on his hind legs with his mouth wide open. "Eugeen, Shelby and Pippin, well I never!" Brutus barked.

Pippin was dancing with Shelby, as there were not enough girls to go around. Their hips wriggled to the music while Eugeen the Afghan playing the piano.

"Just they wait till I see them!" Vader convulsed with laughter.

"Why don't I have testicles like that, in fact why can't I have testicles?" Brutus sighed. Bronte patted him reassuringly and whispered something about "having a big heart instead" to try to make him feel better.

"We can't tell anyone, promise you won't tell anyone?" Bronte begged them.

Momentarily staring at each other and then back to Bronte, Vader replied simply "Yeah, Nah, can't do that sorry!" and then pulled his phone out of his pocket and was taking photographs of Pippin, Shelby and Eugeen through the window. The guilty secret was out or at least it soon would be.

The next day

Bronte was in the kitchen making coffee and toast for herself and Pippin. Not knowing what to say to her brother, she knew that it had to be mentioned because it was only a matter of time before Brutus and Vader told everyone. Even if she could persuade Brutus to keep it quiet, she had no hope of doing that with Vader who spread stories with every bit of drool that came from his mouth.

"Good morning Bronte, is that coffee freshly made?" Pippin walked into the kitchen and without waiting for a response, he poured himself a coffee and picked up a slice of toast from Bronte's plate and stuffed it in his mouth.

"Of course Pippin, you can take my toast if you like I really don't mind." Bronte rolled her eyes and put another slice in the toaster.

Noticing that Pippin looked a bit stiff and sore when he sat down Bronte decided to bite the bullet and ask him how his evening had gone. "How was slimming club at the vets?"

"I told you that I don't need to diet, why would I go to slimming club?" Pippin snapped, completely forgetting what he had told her the night before.

"That's what you told me last night or had that escaped you?" Bronte reminded him.

"Oh I am going to check my Facebook; I shall finish my coffee at my desk as that is the only way I am going to get any peace and quiet around here." Pippin looked uncomfortable because his lies were catching up with him.

"Oh I wouldn't, I think that Facebook is down for maintenance." Bronte insisted but Pippin ignored her and turned on his laptop.

"Oh my days! I have 300 notifications, aren't I a popular boy." Pippin looked smug as he peered at his computer screen.

"The joys of being me, aren't you jealous that you are not me?" He turned around and took a swig of his coffee which a few seconds later was to spurt out of his nostrils and all over his desk.

"Errr Pippin? I am just popping out to see Nica and Gigi." Bronte quickly picked up her mobile phone and opened the door. She didn't get very far, because before the door had a chance to close, she could hear the sound of gasping from her brother which could mean only one thing, he had seen his Facebook and the video that Brutus and Vader had posted.

"What the hell is this? How on earth did this happen?" Pippin screamed and turned around only to see the back of Bronte as she slammed the front door and left.

There on Pippin's Facebook was a video of him in his satin trousers dancing with Shelby and his testicles, with Eugeen playing the piano. I would like to say that it could have been a case of mistaken identity but I would be lying because there was no mistaking Pippin's face, Shelby's testicles and there was certainly no mistaking Eugeen in all of his satin glory.

"Who could have filmed this I wonder?" Pippin seethed. Then as he replayed the video several times, he could hear the unmistakeable sounds of Brutus and Vader snorting with laughter and the gasps of Bronte begging them not to show it.

A few weeks later

'That video' as the gang had named it had a knock on effect for Pippin, Shelby and Eugeen. This wasn't surprising really as it had now gone viral and had been shared on to dog dating sites and was proving to be very popular with the more mature bitches in the rescue kennels.

Shelby and his testicles had found themselves to be very popular and Phoebe had persuaded him to send signed photographs of them to fans.

Eugeen had also been doing pretty well out of it and was in demand to play the piano at weddings, christenings and funerals.

Pippin, who had initially been angry and embarrassed about it, soon changed his mind when he found out that he had been picked to go on 'Celebrity Dancing with Dogs'. This brought so much publicity for the club that he couldn't be angry with Brutus and Vader for long, let alone Bronte who had assigned herself to be his agent.

And talking of Brutus and Vader, after being too scared to show their faces to Pippin for quite some weeks after the whole debacle, they were thrilled when Pippin had appointed them his personal bodyguards.

A few months later at Piney Lakes Reserve

The gang was at Piney Lakes Reserve enjoying one of their special doggy picnics. There was dog chow, dog beer, dog chews to eat and tennis balls to play with, the weather was beautiful and the group was going over their recent successes that had come from 'that video'.

"Well, that escalated quickly didn't it." Shelby raised his glass to make a toast, "To my testicles!"

"Shelby's testicles!" the others raised their glasses and cheered.

"Wish I had testicles like yours," Brutus said enviously.

Shelby patted Brutus on the back and told him that he could be his testicle bodyguard if that would help. This for Brutus was almost as good as winning the Good Boy Award that I invented to make him feel special.

But unbeknown to Shelby, his title of the largest testicles was about to be taken away from him and what is more, he knew nothing about it. In fact, none of them did, well except for Pippin Potter because Pippin knows everything.

The End

CHAPTER TEN

Testicles and Disco Balls

There comes a time in some dogs' lives where he or she may lose their reproductive organs. It is a huge day for them and it involves the Testicle or Ovary Fairy, well don't tell your vet that or they will probably think you are nuts.

This story will give you an insight into this celebratory event and just what happens when the fairies come to visit. One thing is certain; you will never view de-sexing your pet in the same light again.

Pippin Potter's House

Pippin sat at his desk preparing things for the next Iggy play date. Turning around to nibble on his deer antler Pippin was startled by the sound of the phone ringing.

"That will be the phone!" Bronte said without looking up. Lying on her bed, she was busy making notes in her diary.

"Oh I will get that will I?" Pippin said in an unusually sarcastic voice.

"Hello, Pippin Potter here, what? The Testicle Fairy - already? My goodness, this is early."

The Testicle Fairy is a special fairy that once instructed by a human (owners/Vet etc.), takes a dog's testicles as soon as they are old enough so that they can't father any puppies. It is a grand day in a dog's life and they get spoiled after their surgery with toys, treats and cuddles from their owners.

The dogs get a bit nervous and aside from waking up shouting 'where are my balls?' they forget all about it and move on to bigger things to be concerned about like digging holes in the garden and having fun.

Today's turn for the Testicle Fairy was Shelby; it was all sorted and his owners were more worried about the procedure than Shelby was.

"Pippin, when did Brutus lose his testicles?" Bronte asked her brother as he was taking notes for Shelby.

"He had his taken when he was a puppy, although rumours have it they were so large that they were mistaken for oranges but I am not sure how true that is," Pippin replied knowingly.

"I would love to have a set of balls of my own, just for one day of course." Bronte sighed.

Pippin removed his spectacles and chewed them briefly, "You have two tennis balls in the garden, let that be enough for you young lady."

They both laughed and agreed that tennis balls were probably the better option for any dog.

Shelby and the loss of his marvellous testicles

It was a beautiful sunny Friday afternoon and Shelby and Phoebe were at home relaxing with their friends Olivia and her brother Luigi. Phoebe was reading a dog magazine while Shelby was humping Luigi; Shelby didn't care about him being a boy and actually, neither did Luigi come to think of it.

"You don't have to grip me quite so tightly" Luigi wriggled to get away.

"Well, you will have to stay still then!" Shelby said impatiently as his enormous pendulous testicles swung from side to side with every movement.

Shelby's Mum Lara shook her head and sighed. Shelby's behaviour had become too much to manage as Lara was tired of finding naughty dog magazines under his kennel. She was tired of him humping the other boys and when boys were not available, humping his invisible friend called 'Ken'.

Shelby was quite proud of his testicles as you all know and in his bedroom there are lots of photographs in a testicle collage stuck to the wall. Giovanni told Brutus who told Pippin that he actually signs photographs for the girl dogs for a small fee or the odd bone in return.

Phoebe had disappeared into the kitchen to 'help Lara with the cooking', which translates to begging and stealing scraps off the bench.

Lara was chatting on the phone, "Yes of course I shall bring him in tomorrow morning, yes just de-sexing and if you could clip his nails as well that would be good."

That was all Phoebe needed to hear and forgetting about food scraps, she ran back to where the others were, taking the corners so fast that she skidded and almost hit the wall.

"Phoebe what on earth is the matter with you?" barked Shelby,

"Testicle Fairy, he is coming for you tomorrow!" She panted.

Olivia said nothing as the Ovary Fairy had already taken her ovaries a while back; but in sheer sympathy for Shelby, she rolled her eyes to the skies and did a rather dramatic prayer gesture for Shelby's testicles. Shelby spat out his dog chow and looked around at Luigi for clarification.

Luigi scratched his head, "Testicle Fairy, well we knew it was coming old boy, I reckon there is only one thing for it."

Shelby looked at Luigi, "What's that?"

"We need to call Pippin Potter and organise a testicle meeting right away!" Luigi replied.

But Phoebe was already on to it and before Luigi had a chance to instruct her, Phoebe had summonsed an Iggy meeting for the boys at Team Potter's house for later that evening. Of course Pippin already knew as he knows about the Testicle Fairy before anyone else, but there is always a meeting at his house the night before so the dogs can say a blessing for what is about to be lost.

At Pippin Potter's House

Shelby, Giovanni, Dash, Luciano, Carlos, Deejay and Fat Harry had all gathered around the table in Pippin's living room. They were a noisy bunch all trying to talk over one another to get their point across. This happened every time the Testicle or Ovary Fairy visited and only boys or girls were invited to the meeting depending on which fairy was visiting. I mean you wouldn't want boys around if you were discussing girl stuff would you?

Pippin looked around the room and thought it was time for him to do his speech.

Grabbing two stainless steel bowls, he stood on a chair and clanked the bowls together to try to get everyone's attention. "If you could all please be quiet, I need to make an announcement. I would like you all to say a prayer for Shelby's testicles."

Luciano shook his head and said something about it being a 'tragedy' while Giovanni and Fat Harry felt nothing but relief that it wasn't happening to them.

Pursing his lips at the flagrant lack of respect for Shelby's testicles, Pippin snapped, "This is not a laughing matter."

Dash's suggestion to auction Shelby's testicles as doorknockers didn't go down too well with Pippin, while Deejay's shouting that they would make great space-hoppers even less so.

Shelby had covered his ears and was sitting sobbing in the corner apologizing to his manhood. Carlos walked up to him and hugged him "Don't worry my friend, Giovanni lost his nuts and he is still normal."

"That is debatable." Luciano curled his lip as Giovanni poked him sharply in the ribs and called him a 'ball-bag'.

"You are not helping!" Shelby gulped and covered his testicles with a tea towel and briefly wondered if there is life after testicles or would he have to become a girl?

"Can I still have sex with pillows and my invisible friends?" Shelby asked the others.

"Doesn't stop Pippin." Dash gave a dirty laugh.

Pippin said something about humping your invisible friends could be quite fulfilling at times. Deejay had to agree with him, as he was pretty passionate about humping his invisible mates.

Then one by one the Iggies all admitted to doing the same at one time or another. The discussion got so heated that each Iggy started to argue over who had the best invisible friend and whether or not anyone else had humped someone else's invisible friend by mistake.

And before long Shelby felt less nervous about losing his testicles and realised that providing he could still enjoy his sexual relations in whatever form they took, he didn't need his balls in order to do that. Shelby would show the other dogs how it should be done and with such supportive mates, how could he possibly be embarrassed?

The Day of Reckoning (and Testicle Loss)

Shelby sat in the reception area of the vets with his parents as they chatted to the nurse about the procedure. Behind him sat a chunky looking black pug wearing round spectacles sitting with his legs crossed and reading a newspaper. Smiling curtly at the Pug, Shelby was torn between being desperate for some male company and not wanting to talk to a dog with no snout.

The pug buried his head in his newspaper and occasionally peered over the top to see who was in the waiting room. Catching Shelby looking at him, he crouched down further until his newspaper almost covered him like a blanket. Then he slowly peaked up again to see if Shelby was still looking; he was. It was like a game of 'Peek-a-boo' as the little black pug bobbed up and down as though someone was pulling his strings.

"Hello, my name's Shelby." he introduced himself to the pug who was trying to pretend that he wasn't there.

Realising that Shelby wasn't going to leave him alone, the pug looked at him and said, "My name is Spike, pleased to meet you."

"My testicles are coming off today, I am very nervous." Shelby rocked back and forth in his chair to try to comfort himself.

"Same here," Spike replied and quickly covered his mouth with his paws to shut himself up because he had said it aloud so it must be true.

"Does it hurt?" Shelby asked him.

"Don't know, haven't lost my balls before but I don't think so and I have heard that you get lots of treats afterwards."

Shelby felt relieved at the pug's reassurance. Then both he and the Spike sat in a silence that united them with an unspoken connection where both dogs knew what the other was thinking and there was no need to discuss it any further.

Shelby snuggled into his Mum's legs and before he knew it, it was his turn and the vet nurse was calling him in. As she led him to his hospital kennel, Shelby mouthed 'Good luck' to Spike the pug in the waiting room. Spike gave a feeble nod and hid behind his newspaper to go back to being invisible.

The Testicle Fairy's House

The Testicle Fairy was checking his testicle list and like Santa, checking it twice.

"Yep, Shelby and Spike for today," he said to himself and crossed names off his list. "Hopefully I should have enough to make a necklace out of the balls." Within a few minutes, the fairy had disappeared and was to later reappear with a silken handkerchief with the balls wrapped in it.

Later that day

The Testicle and Ovary Fairies were back at the reproductive headquarters discussing the day's events. Now you all know that fairies are tiny little people that only those with a wonderfully creative imagination can see. They always drink out of thimbles and can do magical things with pretty much anything; you just have to believe in them.

"That's nice, where did you get it?" The Ovary Fairy asked the Testicle Fairy, as she sipped wine out of her thimble. She nodded towards two large glittered disco balls in the middle of the room. They were spinning around and catching the light to make pretty colours reflecting off the wall.

"Oh those, they came from Shelby the Iggy and I made them into disco balls." the Testicle Fairy took a mouthful of wine as he admired his own handiwork.

"Oooh my word, they must have made him walk like a cowboy."

"Yep, they sure did and I reckon he will be somewhat lighter for having them removed."

"What about these little ones?" the Ovary Fairy pointed to two tiny little pea sized lumps in a small piece of silk tied around a vase in the middle of the table.

"They are Spike the pugs," the Testicle Fairy replied, "and I plan to use them as knee pads for when I am gardening."

The End

CHAPTER ELEVEN

Pregnancy and Catnip Cigars

Bronte had been behaving strangely and Pippin did not know what to make of it. She had been snappy, complaining about her weight one minute and then crying the next. Poor Pippin was so confused that he had taken to hiding in the wardrobe to escape his moody sister.

"What on earth is the matter with you Bronte?" Pippin sighed.

"You SO would not understand!" Bronte burst into tears and ran out of the room slamming the door, shouting that her life was ruined forever. Pippin shook his head and wondered if all girl dogs were special or if it was just Bronte.

He followed her into the next room where she sat on the bed sobbing that she would soon be fat and none of her clothes would fit her.

Pippin didn't dare say anything; in fact he didn't actually know what to do so he rested his pointy snout on Bronte's back just to let her know that he was there.

"I am pregnant Pippin, I am going to have babies which means that I am going to lose my figure and everything," Bronte wiped her eyes as she turned around to face him.

"Oh my god you are kidding me? I am going to be a father? I can't believe it."

Pippin wasn't actually the father of Bronte's babies (he has been desexed), but let's not ruin it for him because if they live under his roof, then that makes him the Daddy.

"Bronte how exciting! I really ought to tell the gang. How far gone are you, can I hug you?" Pippin gushed.

"Of course you can hug me, they are tiny at the moment." Bronte tried to smile but before she got to say anything else, Pippin had bent down and was talking to her belly.

"This is Pippin here, I am your Daddy and I have big plans for you boys, or girls of course, do you think there are boys and girls in there?"

Bronte rubbed her stomach, "I don't know but these little buggers are making me feel sick, I want to throw up and I am never going to eat again."

"I must go and tell everyone." Pippin grinned. He had heard all about fatherhood and never thought that he would get to pass on his wisdom to his own puppies and now he would get that chance and it was a dream come true for him.

He briefly wondered if he should take some lessons on midwifery, but only briefly as he remembered that he doesn't like the sight of blood, not to mention being squeamish with 'girl stuff'.

A very proud Pippin

Pippin had called a meeting at his house and had summonsed Brutus and as many of the Iggies as he could so that he could tell them his news and Pip could barely contain himself.

Rocco, Nica, Gigi, Fat Harry, Chewy, Georgina and Dash were all wondering what was going on. Nica and Gigi already knew about Bronte as they could sniff out a pregnancy like a sausage in a butchers shop. As for the others, they didn't have a clue.

Rocco was in the corner fighting with himself as usual; Fat Harry kept pointedly looking at his invisible watch to demonstrate that he was hungry. When that failed, he kept pointing to his open mouth while hoping that someone would notice that he had moved into his own personal 'state of hunger'.

It was all going on and Pippin would have to work very hard to get their attention.

"Right you lot, listen up! I have some important news for you!" Pippin attempted to shout but sounded like a softly spoken vicar trying to cheer on the great Lord himself.

"I think you will have to bang a bowl or something," Nica suggested.

Looking around for a dog bowl, Pippin found one and started banging it on the wall with no response. The other Iggies were too wrapped up in their own activities to notice that Pippin was there. Even Brutus hadn't heard him, as he was busy entertaining the younger ones who were making him fart each time they jumped on his belly.

All of a sudden everyone fell silent and looked towards the door. Wondering what they were all staring at, Pippin looked behind him and there was Bronte. She was wearing a navy blue maternity frock with a white pie frilled collar, brown stockings and an Alice band over her ears. "What the bloody hell are you wearing?" Pippin gasped.

Why was Bronte wearing these clothes? I know you are all desperate to know and I shall tell you.

Bronte knew that none of the dogs would listen to Pippin and he could bang food bowls all day and they would just ignore him. But put Bronte in maternity frock, then no words are needed because her clothes do the talking. Nothing shouts 'pregnant' quite like a pie frilled blue maternity frock and brown stockings and an Alice band.

"Oh my god, you are not pregnant are you Bronte?" Zara asked her.

"Oh god, more rugrats to annoy me," Rocco growled and put his head down to wash his bum. He was secretly pleased though; he just didn't want to admit it.

Brutus sat up with his tail wagging, "Puppies! I love puppies; can I be their big brother? I have never been a big brother before."

"Yes, Brutus you can be big brother to my babies," Bronte laughed "If that makes you happy." And it did of course; it made him very happy indeed.

One by one the dogs congratulated Bronte and Pippin, shaking his paw and saying things like 'Well done' and 'We didn't know you had it in you'. Everything was happening so quickly that Pippin wasn't sure how to respond.

"Sorry to do that, but none of them were going to let you speak." Bronte apologised to Pippin.

Pippin told her that it didn't matter at all because nothing could possibly take the shine off this news.

"We absolutely MUST have a baby-shower and I can help you make a list darling. But only designer stuff of course." Gigi said to Bronte who was just nodding to everything she said. "And one more thing darling, it's just a little thing."

"Yes Gigi?" She loved it when Gigi took charge; it was nice and made her feel loved which of course she is and by so many.

"That outfit you have on, well it's not really you is it?" Gigi shook her head vigorously to emphasise the 'NOT' part of the sentence.

Bronte pretended to look offended "Actually I was thinking that it quite suited me," and laughed at the look of horror on Gigi's face and agreed that no, it wasn't her at all.

Pippin was out in the garden with the boys who were asking him how he felt about the news. Blushing from all the attention and admiration from them, Pippin told them that this was an occasion for a cigar and who would like to join him?

The boys in the group all lined up while Pippin handed them a catnip cigar, then one by one, he lit them with matches that he had taken from the kitchen.

"What do I do with this?" Brutus whispered to Rocco.

"Just take a puff and breathe out through your nostrils," Rocco said confidently.

The other dogs were happy to follow Rocco on this and soon they all had their cigars ready to smoke. Once Pippin gave a proud nod, they all took a puff, even though some of them were too embarrassed to admit they had never smoked catnip before.

"Quite good!" Rocco spluttered as smoke came out of his snout and mouth.

"Good stuff Pippin, good stuff." Fat Harry coughed and added in a strained voice "Might go and buy some of these myself."

"Brutus are you OK?" Pippin asked him as he sat by the tree smoking his cigar. Smoke filtered out of his huge nostrils, ears and jowls giving the illusion that he was on fire.

"I don't think I like it." Brutus coughed and then promptly vomited on the floor where Fat Harry not being one to miss an opportunity; quickly gobbled it up afterwards.

At bedtime

The celebrations had finished, the dogs had gone home and all was quiet and peaceful in the Potter house.

Pippin was in bed wearing his half rimmed spectacles reading a book titled 'Impending parenthood' and Bronte was in the garden doing her last pee of the night. Technically every hour was her 'last pee of the night' as she was peeing a lot just like pregnant ladies do. Except that they don't pee in the garden, well they might do but that is their business and who am I to judge.

Bronte walked into the bedroom and saw Pippin tucked up in bed with his book. He looked adorable with the blankets pulled right up to his chin.

"Did you want me to turn the light out Pip?" Bronte asked him.

"No thank you, I want to finish my book as I have to be prepared you see," Pippin replied without looking up.

"What shall we do tomorrow Pippin, shall we look at puppy clothes on the Internet?" Bronte asked him while trying to get comfy in her bed. Pippin didn't answer.

"Pippin did you hear me?" Bronte repeated and still Pippin didn't answer.

Bronte sat up and saw that Pippin had fallen asleep while holding his book. Gently removing his glasses and shutting the book, she nudged him with her snout.

"Thank you Pippin, for being there and just for being you." Curling up next to him, Bronte soon fell asleep where they were both soon dreaming about good things to come and all of it involving puppies.

The End

CHAPTER TWELVE

Pippin becomes a Dad

Bronte was expecting puppies and Pippin was convinced that he was the Daddy. He had taken to wearing tweed, sensible shoes and going to parenting classes to prepare him for fatherhood.

The time was near and Bronte was expected to 'pop' at any given point. Nica and Madame Gigi had been drafted in to be midwives while the rest of the Iggies had been banished to the garden.

Pippin had surprised everyone by asking Brutus to be his support person.

"You want me to do that, really?" Brutus confirmed with Pippin.

Pippin told him that yes, as his right-hand man, he most certainly did want him by his side and they needed to make a birth plan for Bronte's labour. Brutus was so rapt at being asked to be a support person that he barely heard him.

What does a support person do? Brutus didn't know, he knew nothing about puppies except for when he was a baby himself and that was such a long time ago that he couldn't remember it.

Darling Pippin, although he wasn't the real father of the puppies, that didn't matter a jot because he was going to teach them the most important things of all and that was how to be good dogs with respect for their elders.

He would love and treasure the babies until they went to their new homes and he would love and protect Bronte forever and that my friends, is what makes a good Daddy in doggy terms.

Brutus wasn't sure what benefit he could be to Pippin but he figured that it couldn't be that hard and he would just follow Rocco's mantra of 'fake it till you make it'.

A little head appeared from the doorway and Gigi signalled for the boys that Bronte was about to have her puppies.

"Come on Pippin the time has come for you to be a Daddy." Brutus pushed him towards the door.

"Brutus?"

"What's up Pip?"

"Do you think I can do it, be a Daddy I mean?" Pippin looked at Brutus for reassurance.

"Of course you can, you've got this my friend" Brutus said to the quivering little dog.

"Yes, I've got this, I have totally got this" Pippin repeated.

In the maternity crate - where puppies are born

"Pippin and Brutus, you have to come in now," Nica said in a no-nonsense voice.

Bronte was lying in her maternity crate surrounded by flowers, bones and a 21st birthday card from everyone at the Iggy Club. Fat Harry had been sent to buy a 'new puppy' card but picked up the birthday card by mistake; still it's the thought that counts.

"What do I do?" Brutus asked Pippin.

"Not sure, never mind that, what do I do?" Pippin scratched his head and twisted his own ears because he was anxious.

Madame Gigi handed Pippin a squeaky frog to keep him busy and told Brutus to go and find some towels. Not that they needed any towels but it was to keep him out of their way.

"Right, another contraction!" Nica said to Gigi, "Are you ready Bronte?"

"It hurts, I want my Mum, oh my god I SO don't do pain - Nica get these bloody puppies out now!" Bronte yelped.

"Bronte you have to breathe through the contractions! Do that stuff they taught you in maternity class, now start panting!" Pippin told her as he fumbled around for her paw.

"Pippin my love, I wouldn't be saying that kind of stuff to her while she is in labour." Nica tried to warn him.

Ignoring her, Pippin carried on telling Bronte to breathe while doing panting demonstrations to 'help' her get the puppies out.

"I swear to god if you say breathe one more time I shall use your legs as carrots and snap them!" Bronte growled and then said some rude words, which I simply cannot repeat.

"There's no need to be like that!" Pippin said horrified at the language that Bronte was using.

Meanwhile Brutus came running up to Gigi with a blue fluffy towel in his mouth. Happy to be of any use, he carefully placed it on the bed.

"Brutus fetch me another towel," Gigi ordered him. Unknown to Brutus, the girls had hidden towels all over the house to make Brutus feel useful, after all everyone needs to feel needed, especially Brutus.

"OK, first pup is ready to make an appearance." Gigi nodded to Nica who had run out of towels for Brutus to find and had resorted to using Janice Potter's bras as a substitute.

"Brutus, do you know what a bra looks like?" Nica asked him.

Brutus said that yes he did, he had pulled enough off the washing line as a baby although he did consider himself a bit old for such antics now.

"Good, can you go and find one of Janice's bras and bring it to me."

"Right Bronte, you push when I say so, as your first pup wants to come out, OK?" Nica said to her, then turning towards Pippin she barked "Pippin, come here now please, Bronte needs you."

Pippin rushed up to Bronte and gripped her paw. Never had he seen her look more beautiful than she did now and he actually thought his heart might burst with pride at the sight of her.

"I can see the head!" Gigi squealed.

"So can I!" Pippin shouted, 'Brutus, come and see a head, have you ever seen a head before?'

"Puppy coming out!" Gigi barked.

"Brutus! Puppy coming out, come here now!" Pippin was panicking and needed his support friend by his side.

Seconds later the first pup, a boy, made his way into the world, followed by another boy, then three girls.

Just as the last puppy popped out, Brutus turned up panting with one of Janice's bras in his mouth. "Gigi, I have found a bra is this OK......."

Brutus noticed the pile of squirming puppies all fighting to suckle from an exhausted Bronte whose coat was dark with sweat. Next to Bronte was Pippin with his ears sticking out like the handlebars of a bicycle, looking as though he had won the jackpot.

Brutus stood there with the bra still in his mouth. He marvelled at how tiny they were, the noises that they made and he could not believe how anything so small could be quite so perfect.

"Not bad don't you think Brutus?" Bronte smiled weakly.

Unable to speak Brutus dropped the bra on the floor, with tears running down his face, he nodded and squeezed Bronte's paw at the same time.

"Let's leave the happy family alone." Nica nudged Brutus who could not take his eyes off the puppies and wondered if he would be allowed to have one to take home and keep.

Pippin stared at Bronte who had fallen asleep, the puppies were snuggled up to her belly in a wriggling mass of puppy breath, snub noses and puppy squeaks.

He leaned forward and gently touched each one with his snout, doing a quick check to see if they had all their legs and toes (something all new parents do or so my mother told me). Satisfied that they were all in order, Pippin allowed himself a few minutes to stare at his 'children'.

Pippin spent time telling the puppies how much he would love them and what he would teach them and once he had done that, he spent a few more minutes just staring at them because they were so perfect.

A short while later

"So, what is it like being a Dad?" Brutus asked Pippin, he was envious of his little friend because Brutus would never know that privilege.

"I think I am going to like it." Pippin nodded and wiped his eyes and tried to compose himself. The two boys stood there side by side as Brutus placed a paw on Pippin's back, "And I think you are going to be very good at it as well."

In the garden

The Iggies were in Janice's garden eagerly awaiting the news. "Shhhh, they are coming!" Carlos shouted as the others all jostled each other to get to the front.

Pippin came out of the doors with the look that many new fathers have, his chest puffed out and looking a few inches taller from 'walking on air' as they say.

"We have five puppies, Mum and babies doing well," Pippin announced to his group before emotions took over and he burst into tears and as his friends congratulated him, you could hear the sounds of excited barks from several streets away.

It was a King that took to his bed that night in the form of Pippin Potter with his five new responsibilities that would rely on him for protection and guidance.

Pippin was asleep by Bronte's crate as close as he could get without her telling him off. When Janice went to check on him, she found between his paws, a photograph of Bronte with the puppies that Brutus had taken and on the back of the photograph was written 'My family - March 20th 2016'.

The End

CHAPTER THIRTEEN

Daddy Daycare

A few weeks after Bronte had given birth to her puppies, Pippin had assumed the role of the father, which had always been the plan. Bronte was being a superb Mum and would sometimes allow Pippin to fuss the puppies and keep their snouts and bums clean. But Bronte was long overdue a night out with the girls and needed to find a babysitter for the pups.

"I need to find a babysitter tonight so I can go out with Madame Gigi and Nica," Bronte said to Pippin one day. She was nervous about leaving her babies, yet a night out with the girls was much needed because they had plans to talk about how to get your figure back after whelping.

Pippin looked thoughtful, "I can look after the babies."

Bronte looked taken aback "Are you sure? I mean really?"

"How hard can it be?" Pippin replied, "I shall ask Brutus to come around and give me a hand."

Pursing her lips, Bronte looked down at her five chubby puppies looking cute in their bed and wondered if she dare trust her precious children to Pippin and Brutus - especially Brutus, who has no idea as to how big and clumsy he is.

However, there was no time to lose and certainly no time to organise an alternative.

Taking a deep breath Bronte said nervously, "OK, you and Brutus can look after my babies." Then she scurried off before she changed her mind.

Ten Mins Later

"Pippin, does my bum look big in this? Oh my god I can't wait to get my pre-baby figure back and get back into my smart clothes." Bronte checked her bottom out in the mirror.

"You look lovely," Pippin reassured her. Nica had taught him to say that and if that didn't work, to then tell her that she looked like a supermodel.

A loud banging could be heard as the front door rattled causing Pippin to startle.

"That will be Brutus!" Pippin jumped up to get the door. There was no mistaking the large outline through the glass with Brutus's enormous radar-like ears sticking up.

"That will be my babies awake!" Bronte growled and made mental notes to kick Brutus's bum if he woke her children up. As any new mother will tell you, there is nothing worse than a knock at the door or even someone breathing to make you fear your children being disturbed. That in itself can result in an angry mother ready to throat-punch the culprit.

"Hi Bronte! Thank you for letting me puppy-sit with Pippin. Can I see the babies?" Brutus said in his usual deep voice that could give Big Ben a run for its money in terms of decibels.

"Shhhhhh!" Bronte hissed at Brutus and stood aside for him to come in.

"Oh my god, can I have that one?" Brutus squealed in excitement completely oblivious to Bronte glaring at him.

"Are you sure that you boys are going to be OK?" Bronte asked Pippin.

"Yes, yes, we have it covered, anyone would think you didn't trust us" Pippin said confidently, 'I mean it can't be that difficult?'

Grabbing her denim jacket, Bronte took a deep breath and snapped "They had better all be here when I get back!"

And with that, she slammed the door leaving nothing more than a waft of her new perfume 'Eau de ca bitch'.

Let the fun begin

"We've got this covered Pippin, this is going to be easy." Brutus grinned. Pippin was staring at the five puppies wondering what the hell he would do if they woke up.

"I've brought cans of beer," Brutus said and without even looking, he threw a can of dog beer towards Pippin who only just managed to catch it and stop it landing near the puppy cage.

"Careful Brutus! We don't want to wake them now do we?"

But it was too late; Brutus was already leaning over them and talking to them. Desperate for a small brother of his own, he was telling his favourite puppy 'Dumbo' about life and how if he were his brother he would always protect him.

"Brutus what have you done? They are awake now!" Pippin said impatiently and patted the chair to encourage him to sit down.

Brutus quickly ran back to the sofa and tried his hardest to ignore the puppies. Cracking open a beer, they sat down and pretended that they couldn't hear the puppy cries and squeals of 'Dad! Dad!' (Puppies can talk from a very early age you know if you care to listen)

"I'll go and see to them." Brutus jumped up before Pippin could stop him. Scooping up all of the puppies into his big arms, he started singing in a deep and tuneless voice that could frighten God himself.

"Twinkle twinkle smack my bum, if you do I'll tell my Mum." which of course made the puppies start to howl.

"Can't you sing something more soothing?" Pippin flapped his paws in panic.

Holding the puppies, Brutus balanced them so they could see over his shoulder and started bouncing them up and down.

"What on earth are you doing?" Pippin said looking mortified.

"I saw some humans do it in a film once to stop the baby crying," Brutus replied sounding rattled as the puppies howled even louder.

"Sing something else!" Pippin was hyperventilating now at the thought of having all of his puppies awake at the same time.

"Rock a sweet puppy loved by his Mum, give him a sprout and he'll smell from his bum." Brutus found his own toilet humour so amusing that he started to laugh and fart at the same time, which of course jolted the puppies about even more.

"Do all your songs have to have bums in them and can you please stop farting!" Pippin shook his head and grabbed two of the five pups from Brutus. Soon the puppies were squealing so loudly that neither Brutus nor Pippin could shut them up, in fact I am surprised the neighbours didn't complain.

"Pippin, what do we do?" Brutus looked at his friend in desperation while bouncing three of the babies up and down.

"You can stop bouncing them so hard for starters." Pippin barked and carried on walking up and down the front room with the other two puppies in his arms.

"Why is that?" Brutus asked looking the picture of innocence bless him, he doesn't have experience with babies you see.

"Well, because....." Pippin began to say but trailed off just as two of the three puppies puked down Brutus's back, "Bronte only fed them a short while ago." Pippin finished the sentence.

"That is positively disgusting!" Brutus yelled and placed the howling puppies on the floor while he went to wash himself.

"Brutus can you help me with these diapers please as I think there has been some kind of accident." He heard Pippin's voice from the living room.

"Is it worse than vomit?" Brutus asked nervously.

"Hmmm, I will let you decide as I haven't done this before."

Taking a deep breath, Brutus went back into the front room to see Pippin with the puppies lined up on a changing mat with their little bodies wriggling and Pippin trying hard to keep them still.

"Oh my god, is that normal?" Brutus exclaimed making gagging noises.

"I am sure I never produced that," Pippin gasped, "Go on, you go first." and then followed with his own retching noises, which were pretty dramatic.

"Must I?" Brutus swallowed a few times and tried to hold his breath.

"They have to be changed Brutus, that is probably why they were howling." Pippin growled,

"And as you woke them up, you can help me clean them up."

One hour later

"Do you think that will do?" Pippin asked Brutus. Both dogs had talcum powder all over their faces, paws and even their snouts.

"Yes, I think so, not a bad job I must say." Brutus nodded.

"I am tired now, shall we sit down for a quick beer?" Pippin handed Brutus a can. A shocked and traumatised Brutus just nodded, took the beer and collapsed on to the sofa.

Two hours later

"Hi boys, I'm home! Did you miss me?" Bronte quietly opened the front door. She was glad to be home as she had been fretting about her puppies all night. Instead of discussing fashion and figures, she had ended up talking about her babies and showing Nica and Gigi all the baby photos on her mobile leaving them with no alternative but to confiscate it.

(No response from Pippin and Brutus)

"Pippin, Brutus, where are you?" Bronte said a little more loudly. Good God, where on earth were they? She hoped that they hadn't taken them outside; they were not even vaccinated yet.

Chucking her bag on the table, Bronte ran towards her puppy crate. "Oh dear, oh my god, what the hell have they done?" She gasped.

Lying on the sofa was Pippin and Brutus fast asleep snoring loudly. Brutus had three puppies lying across his belly and Pippin had the other two. All of the puppies had their diapers put on the wrong way; all were covered in talcum powder, as were Pippin and Brutus.

Bronte stared at them for a few minutes, then carefully and one by one, removed the puppies from the boys and placed them back in their puppy crate.

Should she wake them up and tell them that they messed up? No perhaps she shouldn't, after all they might not make puppy-sitters of the year but they had tried their best and the puppies looked peaceful enough.

Brutus was twitching in his sleep with his huge tail wagging and whacking a sleeping Pippin in the face. Bedtime story books lay scattered about the living room also covered in talc; the whole place looked a mess.

"All is well that ends well." Bronte thought and picked up a large blanket to cover them both as they slept.

"Puppies, where are the puppies?" Brutus growled in his sleep.

"What time is it?" Pippin asked in a drowsy voice.

"Time to sleep Pippin, time to sleep." Bronte smiled at her brother.

"Is everything OK? Did we look after them OK?" Pippin rubbed his eyes.

Staring around at the mess and the sleeping puppies with diapers on the wrong way around, Bronte nodded "Yes, everything is fine and you boys did just great."

Adjusting the blanket that covered Brutus and Pippin, Bronte switched the light off and went to the puppy crate. But not before she took a quick photo to send to Nica and Gigi for a piss take in the morning.

The End

CHAPTER FOURTEEN

Family Reunion

At Phoebe and Shelby's house

It was a day where Phoebe was feeling unsettled and she had found solace in pestering Shelby and generally being annoying. You know how it is when you want to make your own entertainment and your siblings are not interested, it's amusing to irritate them until you get a reaction.

"Shelby, do you wanna play a game of bitey-face?" Phoebe pestered him.

Telling her that no, he did not want to play a game of bitey-face and could she please be quiet so he could finish his newspaper, Shelby shook his head and prayed for silence.

"Shelby?" Phoebe repeated with a high-pitched whine.

"Yes, Phoebe what do you want?" Shelby sighed, he had been reading the same paragraph in the newspaper for ten minutes and was getting impatient.

"Do you ever wonder about your family and if you have any other brothers and sisters and where they are living?" She asked him.

"No, I don't suppose I do." Shelby snapped without looking up and carried on reading his newspaper.

"Be like that then." Phoebe slapped Shelby's newspaper with her paw and trotted off to ask her Mum Lara about tracing her family tree, or was it a family bush? Phoebe could never remember so perhaps it was a bush after all.

"Phoebe, why do you want to trace your family?" Lara asked her while spooning a couple of teaspoons of coffee into a mug.

Phoebe cocked her head to the side and said she didn't know why but she just knew that something was missing in her life and perhaps it was a blood brother or sister aside from Shelby.

"Oh well, if you insist." Lara made a note on her 'To Do' list to contact the breeder to ask her if she knew anything.

A Week Later

Lara had gone to get the post, gripping some envelopes in her hand from the mailbox, she quickly flicked through them "Probably bills, that's all we seem to get these days." She was about to place them on the counter to open later, when she spotted an envelope with Phoebe's breeder's handwriting on the front. It was the results of Phoebe's pedigree and lineage. Without hesitation, she ripped open the envelope and read it, and then she read it again just to make sure.

"Phoebe, could you come to the kitchen please."

"What's up, Mum?" Phoebe came running in and skidded along the floor hitting the table leg as she spotted the letter from the breeder.

"Well, it appears you have a brother." her Mum patted Phoebe on her rump.

"A brother aside from Shelby? Are you serious?" Phoebe's eyes were almost popping out of her head.

"Yes, I am serious." Lara waved the letter at Phoebe.

"Who? Where?" Phoebe said in a shrill voice.

"Would you like to meet him and would you like to go now?" Lara picked up her car keys because she already knew the answer to that one.

"Oh my god, can we?" Phoebe gulped, "Do you think he will want to meet me?"

"Get your leash ready, I just have to make a quick phone call," Lara said to Phoebe who skidded out of the kitchen with her long legs tripping up giving the illusion that she had at least 8 of them (legs).

Lara made sure that Phoebe had gone and picked up her phone; taking a deep breath she dialled a number and waited a few seconds for an answer. "Hi there, yes it's me, can I come around, I have some news for you."

At Pippin Potter's House

Pippin was furious because Bronte had left him with the puppies so that she could 'do lunch' with Madame Gigi and Nica. Of course the kids were running rings around him and driving him nuts.

"Dumbo, will you stop that right now!" Pippin shouted as Dumbo nipped his ankles and called him 'smelly bum'.

The five puppies all had names now and were full of mischief. They had peed on Pippin, shit on his blanket, they then sang the song of their people to wake him up and had taken to chewing his ears despite having baby teeth.

"Whoever said that rearing children is easy never had this lot!" Pippin growled as he tidied up Bronte's puppy crate. No wonder that Bronte had been so keen to go out and get five minutes to herself.

Turning around to leave the cage, he saw two of the puppies Latte and Dumbo waddle off giggling. Trying the cage door he saw that he had been locked in.

"Dumbo this is not funny, open this door now! Do as you are told, I am your father and you should have more respect" Pippin demanded and sat there helplessly as the five puppies ran amok in the living room while he could only watch them.

I think mutiny would have broken out had the phone not rang which was promptly picked up by Pippin's Mum Janice.

131

"Hi there, how lovely to hear from you. Yes, they are not too bad but still managing to drive old Pippin mad. Of course you can, see you shortly." Janice said to whoever was on the phone. She was trying to keep an eye on the puppies and make sure that they didn't squeeze into anything they shouldn't which at this age was pretty much everything.

"Oh Pippin, how did you get in there you silly boy!" Janice laughed and let him out of his cage. Pippin ran after the puppies and told them not to be so childish and how they should have more respect. The puppies argued that it wasn't their fault that they were so naughty.

"But we are only children Dad, we are meant to be childish." Dumbo piped up as his siblings nodded in agreement. Pippin told them to wait until Bronte got home and then they would be sorry.

This is the one threat made by parents that can scare the crap out of you. The very words 'Just you wait till your Mother/Father gets home', is enough to make you hide under the bed because you just know you will get told off big time.

Pippin had calmed down enough to put on his 'Dad Cardigan'. This is a waffle knitted beige cardigan that all new Dads wear and one pocket always has tissues stuffed in it.

Giovanni told Pippin that by wearing the 'Dad Cardigan', it would give him authority and magic powers to be able to do 'Dad stuff'. Giovanni should know because he is a Dad several times over.

Mind you, I have never seen Giovanni wearing a waffle knit beige cardigan.

If any of your human male friends are about to become a father, be sure to buy them a waffle knitted beige cardigan and fill the pockets with tissues. No really, they will thank you for it

"Pippin I have some news for you, can you come here please?" Janice shouted to Pippin from the kitchen.

"Coming Mum, love you Mum," Pippin replied. Brutus had taught him to end every sentence to his Mum with 'Love you Mum' because it cancels out any wrong doing that you might have done, after all, who can resist the words 'Love you Mum'?

Pippin sat in front of Janice while wagging his tail "Yes Mum?"

"I have found out today that you have a sister living in Perth," Janice told him.

Pippin swallowed a few times, looked around the room and then back at Janice "A sister? My sister? Are you sure?"

"Yes, positive." she replied.

Pippin looked shocked, I mean you all know that he is a family dog but having it sprung on him that he has a sister that he has never met, well that is a huge deal and he actually felt quite emotional.

"When can I meet her?" He asked nervously.

"Right now" Janice grinned as the doorbell rang.

Hiding behind his little bed, Pippin felt sick. Would she like him? What would she think? Would they get on? So many questions and there was no time to worry because he was about to get them answered.

As Janice answered the door, Pippin saw Lara through the glass and wondered what she was doing at his house. Was it an Iggy play date that he didn't know about? Highly unlikely as Pippin not only knew about every Iggy play date, he actually organises all of them.

"Hi Janice, thanks ever so much for having us, I can't believe it can you?" Lara laughed as she sat down while Janice put the kettle on to make a cup of tea.

"Phoebe! What are you doing here? I have some news, you will never guess what it is!" Pippin wagged his tail because he was so excited.

"I have news as well." Phoebe barked back and gave Pippin a hug.

"I have a sister in Perth." Pippin blurted out as emotions got the better of him. He had to fight back the tears, which made his little voice go all wobbly as he tried to contain himself.

"Well fancy that, what a coincidence as I have a brother in Perth as well, do you think they might know each other?" Phoebe said as she gave the puppies in the crate a quick wave to acknowledge them.

"Here you go you two, have a read of this." Lara handed the letter to Phoebe and Pippin.

"Let's sit outside and leave these two alone as they have heaps to talk about," Janice said to Lara and nodded towards the garden.

Pippin and Phoebe huddled up over the letter, both dogs were silent but their mouths moved a little as they read through the paperwork.

"Oh my god really?" Phoebe gasped.

"It seems that way," Pippin whispered.

They read it again, looked at each other and then read it again.

"This is pretty awesome," Phoebe said to Pippin.

"Yes, yes it is, sister!" Pippin laughed and gave Phoebe a playful poke in the ribs.

"Don't you poke me, brother!" Phoebe responded.

Pippin and Phoebe stared at each other, totally oblivious to the puppies that were peeing on each other's heads in the crate.

In the garden

Janice and Lara were sat outside having their coffee. "Do you think they are OK?" Lara asked Janice.

"Let me go and check." Placing her coffee mug on the table, Janice got up and went to the house and peered around the corner to see if it had all gone OK. Pippin is a very sensitive little dog and the shock could really upset him.

"Pippin, are you OK?" Janice's voice trailed off.

For there in Pippin's bed was Phoebe and Pippin curled up together with the puppies, both of them taking it in turns to tell them stories.

Janice watched quietly for a few minutes and marvelled at how they had the same mannerisms and little habits. They laughed at each other's jokes and made the same gestures, how did she not notice it before?

"How are they doing Janice, is everything OK?" Lara asked her when she reappeared in the garden a few minutes later.

"Everything is just fine, wonderful in fact. Now would you like another coffee?" Janice took Lara's cup and smiled at her before putting the kettle on again for another cuppa, two of many that were drunk that day.

Because there was no need to rush home, not today anyway.

The End

CHAPTER FIFTEEN

The Hardest Goodbye

Obviously the hardest part of having puppies, is having to say goodbye to them when they go to their new homes. Bronte's babies were now ready to go to their new owners and had just a few days left with Bronte and Pippin.

Pippin had been subdued ever since he found out that the puppies were going. He had enjoyed being a Dad to them and teaching them his values and other doggy stuff. He had told them stories about lure coursing, Iggy parties and how he came to be Neuter Champion at the dog show.

He had told them about how he was a police dog and had chased criminals, carried a gun and protected his Queen and Country. The puppies eagerly listened to the stories and believed every word. Which of course made Pippin want to exaggerate by saying how he fought in the war, had travelled the world and killed wild bears in Alaska.

Stories that may not have been true but to the puppies, they were the greatest stories ever told and would be ones that they too would tell their children when they were old enough to have them. But before you laugh, didn't you have a parent or grandparents that told you stories about themselves? I know I did, my Dad told me that God had told him to build a church so he built one in St Albans, Hertfordshire - but that is yet another story that I can save for later.

Bronte watched Pippin with the puppies; they were chewing his ears and climbing over him, as he was demonstrating how he fought the wolves in Canada on his own and the Caucasian Shepherd dogs in Russia.

They were so happy role-playing Pippin's stories that Bronte didn't have the heart to tell them to pack their toys and stuff so that they could be ready to go to their new homes.

She was scared of upsetting them and more to the point, scared of upsetting Pippin as well. Taking a deep breath, Bronte walked over to where they were all playing, "Kids, can I have a quick word please and you as well Pippin?"

Pippin looked up at her. He was proud of his family especially Bronte for giving him the chance to help with the babies and send them out into the world with his morals.

Except that the bit about 'sending them out into the big wide world' seemed to have conveniently escaped him, probably because he knew how much it would hurt him when they went so in Pippin's eyes, denial was not just a river in Egypt.

The puppies looked up at Bronte and ran towards her, all jostling for position to get to their Mum as their tubby little bodies all tripped over in their haste to get there. Pippin followed them and was joking with two of the pups about how he used to sing in a boy band called 'ABCD' and was a positive whizz at head banging and playing the air guitar.

"Mum, Daddy said he was singing with the alphabet as a rock star, is that true?" Dumbo asked Bronte.

"I think you mean ABCD." Bronte laughed as Dumbo mouthed the words to get them clear in his head, oh well; they were all letters of the alphabet weren't they?

"Kids come here please, I have some news for you." The puppies listened to Bronte as she broke the news to them that in a couple of days they would be going to their new homes. They looked up at their beloved Pippin, wondering if he could 'save them.' They loved their Dad and did not understand why they had to go anywhere else.

Pippin looked at Bronte accusingly and whilst he remained composed, inwardly he wanted to scream that no, they could not take his precious puppies away from him.

Then without saying anything at all, Pippin turned his back on Bronte and went into the next room to be on his own, leaving his puppies wondering what they might have done to upset him.

"Dad! Dad! Where are you going Dad?" Dumbo cried and one by one, the babies all stumbled after Pippin with their little legs trying desperately to keep up with him.

Bronte wanted to follow him but knew it was his moment to have in order to learn to cope with what was coming.

In the spare room with Pippin

Pippin sat on his bed with his pointy snout between his paws. His heart was breaking and he didn't understand why his babies had to leave. He just couldn't get why he couldn't keep them all for himself. After all when you add up five puppies and two Iggies you still don't have 'much dog' in the house, not really.

"Dad! There you are!" The puppies pushed their way into where Pippin was. Pippin was broken; this was different to anything he had ever felt before because there is nothing as painful as saying goodbye to the ones you love.

Looking up at the puppies, Pippin beckoned for them to curl up next to him and within seconds they were playing 'bitey-face' and wagging their little tails in circles as Pippin blew raspberries on their tummies and pretended they were farts.

"Dad, can you sing one of your rock songs again for us?" the puppies pleaded with him, "And can you play the air guitar for us like last time?"

Pippin laughed and started singing ABCD songs, only he didn't know the words so made his own up and pretended to play the air guitar. He had told the puppies that you can buy air guitars in all the shops but they are so expensive that only special people can afford them because they pay with their imagination instead of cash. He kind of has a point on that one I reckon.

Bronte was watching from the door as Pippin was dancing with the pups and singing songs while the puppies jumped and barked beside him. Should she go in and see how they were all handling it, perhaps not.

Quietly shutting the door behind her, she left them alone to continue being rock stars playing with fantastic invisible instruments, while being caught at a magical point in time that they would never get back.

"But why Daddy, why can't we stay with you?" the Dumbo asked Pippin.

Pippin took a big breath, "Because you have parents waiting to love you as much as we do and you wouldn't want to take that away from them would you?"

The puppies cocked their heads to the side to take it all in, "Will we still be able to sing alphabet songs and play the air guitar?"

Pippin laughed, "Yes you can do all of that not to mention enjoy all the toys and treats that you will get from your new parents.

"Plus don't forget we may still get to see each other at Iggy club events and the famous Furbaby Cafe when we have our parties."

And that was enough to placate the five anxious puppies. Sadly however, that left a distraught Pippin Potter who very quickly had to put on his 'big boy collar' and get tough because very soon he was going to have to say goodbye to his babies and have his heart broken.

Time to go

The day had arrived for the five puppies to go to their new homes. Their breeder, Joanne was coming to pick them up to take them to her house and their new parents would be collecting them from there.

Pippin had resigned himself to the fact that they were going, he didn't like it and had rather likened it to vomiting; it would hurt but had to happen and he would feel better in the end.

"Pip, aren't you coming to say goodbye?" Bronte asked Pippin who was hiding in the puppy crate clinging on to a blanket.

"No, it's OK, they don't need me; you can go." He said without even looking up.

Bronte felt upset at these words and not knowing what to say to change his mind, she left him alone with his thoughts.

"Is Daddy coming?" the puppies looked expectantly at Bronte.

"Daddy is busy but he loves you all very much." Bronte guided the puppies to the car for Joanne to load them up. "Oh Pippin you daft old boy, cutting your nose off to spite your face." Bronte thought.

"We want our Daddy!" Shouted the puppies and pressed their tiny button noses against the window making their unique 'nose-art' on the glass.

"Thanks Janice, I will call you to let you know how it goes." Joanne nodded as she started to pull out of the driveway.

"Hold on Joanne wait for me, it's me!" it was the unmistakeable voice of Pippin with his BBC English accent. The little dog ran with all his might and bolted out of the house and much to Janice's horror proceeded to jump the fence and run straight after Joanne's car.

"Is that Daddy?" one of the pups barked to the others. They all looked out of the window and saw Pippin frantically trying to catch the car, with his pointy snout opening and closing mouthing the words "Stop, it's Pippin!"

"It's our Daddy! We knew he wouldn't forget us!" the puppies squealed and cried to the point that Joanne couldn't ignore them.

"What on earth are you lot doing?" Joanne checked in her rear view mirror, "Oh my goodness, that's Pippin, has he escaped?"

Slamming on the breaks, Joanne got out of the car and before she had a chance to close the driver door, an exhausted and breathless Pippin Potter leapt into her car and straight into the back with the puppies where he proceeded to cry. He cried because he felt bad that he never said goodbye, he cried because he was going to miss them and finally he cried because he was now genuinely happy that they were going to wonderful new owners.

"Oh Joanne, Pippin was chasing after you!" Janice gasped as she ran up to the car and leaned on to the bonnet to catch her breath.

Joanne and Janice looked through the window to see Pippin hugging and kissing each pup, making them promise to be good dogs and to always practice the air guitar before bed while singing the song of their people.

"Do you think he will be OK?" Janice asked her.

Watching Pippin who was in the back of the car talking to the puppies, Joanne smiled, "He is going to be just fine."

And with that Janice had to be content because Joanne just knew these things and was rarely wrong about them.

"Right then kids, let's get you to your new owners, they will be wondering where I have got to," Joanne shut the car door. Then turning around to Pippin, she patted his head affectionately, "Catch you later Pippin."

Pippin gave a curt nod and composed himself. He was still out of breath from his little car chase but that could constitute his exercise for a week, well at least that was what he planned to tell his Mum anyway.

Janice was staring at the vehicle as it disappeared up the road, just in time to see five tiny bottoms with their bums pressed against the back window leaving 'bum marks' on the glass.

"Pippin did you teach them that?" But Pip had gone inside to catch up with Bronte leaving Janice quietly chuckling to herself and wondering what other naughty delights he had taught them.

In bed that night

Pippin and Bronte were curled up in their beds and all evidence of the puppies had been cleared up. Things were back to normal and 'Daddy Pippin' had been put back in its box along with the brown waffle knit 'Dad cardigan', and 'normal Pippin' was back.

"Does it get any easier Bronte, saying goodbye I mean?"

Bronte was quiet for a few minutes before she gave her answer, "Not really, I always miss them when they first go. But it is good to catch up with them again if they stay local."

"If it hurts, why do you do it? Why do we do it?" Pippin asked her.

Said Bronte, "It's the circle of life Pippin, that's just how it is and we let them go to good homes not because we don't care, but because we do.

"By the way, you were so brave, I was proud of you today Pippin."

"Yes, I think I was rather brave actually." Pippin agreed.

He couldn't wait to tell Brutus about the day's adventures either. Only he would tell him that he ran all the way to Joanne's house, chasing the car along the freeway and overtaking road trains. Just for effect of course, because Brutus believes everything he is told.

The two dogs finally settled down for the night and curled up on their beds together. Apart from giving the odd sigh of contentment, nothing more could be heard other than the sound of them giving gentle snores as they slept.

The End

CHAPTER SIXTEEN

When Good Dogs Go Bad

Pippin Potter is a quiet little dog, he is clean living and reads respectable dog magazines and the naughtiest stuff he ever does is roll in some horse turd when he gets the chance. Basically he is an all round good boy who is obedient and does twirls for treats.

But being good is all well and 'good' but sometimes, just sometimes we all need to go off the rails a bit and taste a bit of the naughty life and one day, Pippin Potter much to the surprise of his friends, did just that.

Bronte, Nica, Gigi, Olivia and Zara were having a girls evening at Bronte and Pippin's house. This involved discussions about the hottest police dogs, talking about bones and the latest fashion in dog coats.

"When will I be grown up enough to wear short dresses like Bronte?" Olivia asked impatiently. Olivia like Zara is a typical teenage dog that wants to grow up before her time, plays loud music and likes the world to know that she is around.

"You won't be wearing those for a while yet young lady," Gigi said firmly, she was very strict on the younger girls keeping their modesty and Olivia was far too young to be flashing her bottom.

"Hold the fun girls, I must go for a quick pee, won't be a minute," Nica jumped up to go to the garden, but abruptly stopping in her tracks, she gasped "Oh My God, what the hell are you thinking of Pippin?"

Pippin stood by the door wearing a pair of tight jeans, a black leather jacket and a white T-shirt and the picture was complete with him noisily chewing gum with his mouth open. Pippin by the way hates chewing gum citing it as 'common and trashy' and is always lecturing the other Iggies about just how bad it looks.

But now he was actually chewing gum in the insolent fashion that he so hates. Standing with his chest puffed out and his legs wide apart, "Yeah, what of it?" Pippin said to Nica in a newly acquired voice with attitude.

"Erm, well, nothing, nothing at all." Nica backtracked and then ran back to where Bronte was sitting, "You need to come here and quickly."

"Stay here you kids," Bronte told Olivia and Zara who completely ignored her and followed her to see what the fuss was all about.

"Uncle Pippin! What are you wearing?" Zara pointed at him.

"You told us that chewing gum is bad manners, didn't he Zara?" Olivia barked.

"Bronte, do something." Madame Gigi begged her.

"You look daft Pippin, utterly ridiculous." Bronte shook her head and then burst out laughing until the tears poured down her cheeks.

A sound of a car horn could be heard outside and Pippin glared at them, "Catch ya later, I am off out and ladies, I plan to get super drunk so don't wait up."

"Pippin, what has happened to you?" Bronte asked him.

"I just got naughty, that's what." Then he walked out of the house slamming the door behind him.

Gigi peaked out of the window and saw him get in a car where Brutus, Rocco, Chewy and Vader the boxer were waiting.

"Come on man, let's hit the road," Brutus said impatiently as he sat in the back seat of a tatty old car that Vader had borrowed from a friend of a friend who pinched it from a wrecker's yard.

Pippin jumped in the front beside Vader who was driving. While Chewy, Rocco and Brutus sat in the back as rock music blasted out on the car stereo. As they all chewed on their gum and smoked catnip cigarettes, the boys took Pippin on what was to be his first journey of naughtiness.

In a skimpies bar somewhere in town where the bitches don't wear collars

Pippin did not approve of skimpies bars; he always said that nice dogs didn't do that kind of thing, so for him to be persuaded to go to one was a miracle. This particular bar was situated near the local dogs' home, giving the resident female dogs a chance to earn some cash to pay their council registration fees.

As none of the boys had been there before, they were nervous about it and were not sure what to expect. This was made worse because they were frisked over by a well-muscled Doberman before they were allowed inside.

"I say that dog has just assaulted me." Pippin quickly pulled out a tiny bottle of hand sanitizer from his pocket and made a big gesture of squirting some on his paws and rubbing them together, "Who does he think I am, some kind of pervert?"

"We are in a skimpies bar Pippin, what do you expect?" Chewy responded and flicked his long red fur back because it was in his eyes.

Before they had a chance to discuss the definition of the word pervert, Vader and Rocco had gone to the bar to order their drinks to give them some Dutch courage.

"Here's to being naughty!" Rocco raised his glass as the others joined him and clinked their glasses together before drinking their dog beers back in one hit and belching afterwards.

"Pardon me." Brutus apologised and then belched again.

"Excuse me but I still feel sober and this place still looks like a dirty kennel." Pippin stared at the bottom of his beer glass looking for answers, secretly thinking that this naughty life was perhaps not for him and maybe he should go home. OK, one more drink and then he would go home.

Several drinks later

"Nice snout!" Pippin hollered to a blue whippet bitch that was dancing on the tables next to them. Eyeing her up appreciatively, Pippin tucked a dog biscuit into her collar.

"Hello there cutie-pie." the whippet smiled back and then wriggled her butt for Pippin to admire.

Pippin had no idea as to how to behave or what to expect in a skimpies bar. The more nervous he became, the faster he chewed his gum until he nearly choked on his own tongue. Several whippets and a chunky beagle in a bikini were strutting their stuff on the podium. The beagle was searching for food as she danced and would go to full lengths to get treats tucked into her bikini bottoms.

Brutus, Chewy and Rocco were drinking shots, Vader wasn't as he was driving, but he was over excited and had started to fart causing the whippets to wrinkle their noses in disgust.

"Have you shit your pants?" one of the whippets shouted at Vader which prompted him to check his own pants to confirm that no, he hadn't.

"Hey big boy, fancy a dance?" the chunky beagle bitch winked at Pippin and insisted that he step up to the podium with her.

"Go Pippin!" Brutus, Rocco, Vader and Chewy chanted to encourage him, not that he needed any encouragement of course. The boys shoved

Pippin on to the podium to join the dancing beagle who was quickly sneaking a hamburger into her mouth and tucking it inside her jowls for later.

Three large German Shepherd Dog security officers with testicles the size of grapefruits, watched Pippin as he danced next to the beagle. He was now exceedingly drunk and was belching in between trying to keep his chewing gum in his mouth.

"Watch him." One of the GSDs said to the other as they eyed him up suspiciously.

"He is OK mate, he won't get rowdy we promise." Brutus tried to reassure them just before Pippin caused the evening to end quite abruptly.

"Oi boys, it's time for some crowd surfing!" Pippin yelled and before anyone could stop him, he threw himself into a small crowd of dogs that included a pug, a Schnauzer and a rather smelly greyhound with no teeth while taking the bikini bottoms off the beagle bitch at the same time.

"Ouch!" winced Brutus.

"That has gotta hurt." Vader sucked air through his teeth and shook his head.

"Where is Chewy?" Rocco asked as he looked around for the little Tibetan spaniel.

"Will someone for the love of God come and help me!" a little voice came from underneath Pippin. There lying under Pippin's bottom was a rather angry and indignant looking Chewy and not because he had been squashed, but because his hair had been messed up.

"You lot get out now!" the GSD snarled and roughly pulled Pippin up who was really too drunk to go anywhere on his own.

The other security guard spotted Rocco having a fight with his invisible friend. Rolling on the floor and punching fresh air while calling it a 'wanker' Rocco was so wired that he ended up pulling his own ears.

"What the hell is he doing?" the GSD shouted to Brutus.

"He is fighting his invisible friend and you had better watch it because if he gets you then your arse is grass!" Brutus growled and wiped his teeth dry so that he could stick his lips onto them to try to look aggressive.

"Yeah, arse is grass." Vader added as he hid behind a wall post for protection, while Chewy mouthed the words "Shut the hell up." to try to keep the boys quiet.

"Get them out now!" snarled the owner, a very important looking red cloud kelpie with an Australian flag neckerchief tied round his neck. He had been sitting in a leather chair by the stage watching the entire thing unfold.

Within seconds Brutus, Pippin, Chewy, Vader, Rocco and his invisible friend found themselves being picked up by their collars and thrown out of the bar and the last thing they heard was the beagle bitch demanding to know who had stolen her knickers.

"Well, that was an over reaction I must say." Brutus protested to Vader who clutched his nose, as he wanted to snort so badly.

"That was fun." Pippin slurred. As the colour ran from his face, he projectile vomited all over the floor, "I don't feel very well, I want my Mum."

"He's pissed." Vader said knowingly to Brutus, "I can just tell."

"Get him to the car before those bouncers bash the crap out of us." Brutus panicked.

"I am never going out with you lot again, you have completely shamed me!" Chewy said looking offended by the entire evening.

And all Rocco could say was "Everyone is a bastard and I hate you all."

Back in the car

"I think I prefer the sensible Pippin." Chewy barked in the back of the car.

"Yeah, so do I." Rocco agreed.

"Brutus can you have a look at what is stuck on my head please?" Chewy put his head close enough for Brutus to check.

"Chewing gum, how did that get there?" Brutus looked puzzled.

"Has anyone seen my chewing gum?" Pippin said drowsily from the front passenger seat of the car and Chewy's response was as you can imagine, quite rude.

The morning after the night before and the nausea that goes with it

Pippin woke up thinking that he had died, in fact he was sure of it. He never knew that the room could spin so violently and was so scared that he gripped his blankets while secretly praying to God to make it all stop (we have all done that at some point I am sure).

Too scared to open his eyes, he took deep breaths to stop himself from vomiting. Managing to partially sit up, he noticed that he was still wearing his leather jacket, T-shirt and tight jeans and he also noticed that he was utterly filthy, covered in mud and was aching all over.

"Good morning naughty brother, I hope you have got that all out of your system because this high-jinx really isn't becoming of you." Bronte said cheerfully as she barged into Pippin's room and tugged the curtains open causing Pippin to cover his eyes and shout "Jesus Christ!"

"Chewy is absolutely furious about the chewing gum incident; Brutus told me all about it.

"Anyway, here's a coffee to make it all better, coffee solves everything you know," Bronte said to Pippin. She slapped the cup and saucer beside his bed and left the room leaving a waft of her perfume.

Taking a mouthful of the scalding coffee, he tried not to vomit. He felt dreadful; perhaps this bad boy stuff was not for him and especially the chewing gum. As for the beagle knickers, we shall say no more about it as from what I have heard, they still haven't been found.

The next day

Bronte was on her way out for a play date with Gigi and Nica, just the grown ups for a change. Dressed in her shortest dress she was quite pleased with her appearance and gave herself an admiring glance as she passed a mirror.

"Surely you are not going out in that short dress are you?" A voice could be heard from the living room.

Turning around, she saw Pippin at his desk wearing his usual sensible brown collar, his spectacles at the end of his nose and no sign of any chewing gum. He was busy preparing for the next Iggy party while trying very hard not to give into the craving for a bacon sandwich, which often goes hand-in-hand with a hangover.

Bronte felt relieved that he was back to normal, he could leave the naughty stuff to the others thank you very much because she loved him just the way he was.

"You are so sensible!" Bronte laughed and then kissed Pippin on the cheek, "But I wouldn't swap you for the world." Pippin removed his spectacles and started to huff on the lenses and clean them with his handkerchief.

"Nothing wrong in being sensible." Pippin gave an embarrassed smile and went back to his computer and while the title of being sensible suited him just fine, he at least knew that he could be a rebel in a leather jacket if he wanted to.

After all, we all have our own inner rebel that needs to be let out occasionally don't we?

The End

CHAPTER SEVENTEEN

Rainbow Bridge

Rainbow Bridge is the place that our pets go to once they die. It is a place where they regain their health, youth and vitality, where there are no dangers and nobody ever gets hurt. There is always enough space for all those that cross the bridge and most importantly, sore joints, age and illness are left behind.

There is a path, which leads to the gates of Rainbow Bridge, and a big white greyhound called Bowie who is known as the 'Gatekeeper of the Bridge' guards the gates. As all the animals need guidance upon entry and to be advised of protocols, Bowie is the dog to help them with his calm, placid and reassuring nature, which makes the transition period easier.

Once an animal leaves his/her human, whatever pain that may have been plaguing them or however they leave this world, they leave it all behind the very moment they step behind the gates and that is the place where they get to live their lives again.

Rainbow Bridge is a very busy place, there are bones to be eaten, toys to play with and balls to chase. In fact, every little thing that every single dog loves to do in life is provided for its residents. Happiness is free, love and attention in abundance and it really is just a nice place to live.

How do you know when the time is right to send your pet to Rainbow Bridge?

You look into your pet's eyes and you do this over a period of days or weeks and if you really look and bypass the pain that you are feeling and your reluctance to let them go, you will see what they are feeling and the look that they give you will tell you when they have had enough.

Some owners can't or won't see it because it is too emotionally painful and they want to keep their pets right until the last possible moment, which is not always fair on the animal. I wouldn't judge anyone for this, because knowing when to call it a day with your pet and end their suffering is one of the hardest things that a pet owner can do and it is also one of the kindest.

Netty's story

Netty was an elderly terrier that lived at home with her Iggy brother Fletcher and their human family. Old age had slowly crept up on her and had started to 'steal' her health, vitality and mobility and overall joy for life and living.

"Are we there yet dear?" Netty would frequently ask her owners whenever she was feeling lost, to which they would reply "Not yet Netty, not yet."

One day Netty was in her bed at home, Fletcher was sitting on the chair and it seemed a normal morning just like any other.

Except that it wasn't, it was to be the day that Netty would cross over to Rainbow Bridge.

"Fletcher?" Netty asked her brother.

"Yes, Netty?"

"I think it is time." Netty nodded at him and rested her head on her paws.

Fletcher said nothing but he knew what she was talking about and had known for a while that this day was coming. After a few minutes, he said, "I agree, let's tell Mum. She will know what to do for the best, she always does."

All animals know the saying; 'I think it's time' it is like an inbuilt body clock that tells every single animal in the world when it is time to leave this life and no explanation is needed.

Time is the only thing that is really important to animals aside from the people that love them. Time comes in many forms for instance bedtime, dinnertime, bath time, time for the vet, playtime and finally 'It's time' as in time to go to Rainbow Bridge.

Animals don't need clocks because the one they have in their hearts, heads and stomachs tells them all that they need to know.

Anyway, back to Netty.

Netty's owners Iris and Mike came and sat with her to see if she was OK and it was clear to them that she wasn't.

"Are we there yet?" Netty asked her Mum and Dad, looking at them with her cloudy eyes that struggled to focus.

Iris looked at her husband, no words were needed as their eyes connected with each other and then connected with Netty. They both knew what they had to do which was to give Netty her wings to allow her to go to Rainbow Bridge. "Nearly Netty, nearly there."

Fletcher stared at his sister, he felt sad but he knew it was for the best and that once she was at Rainbow Bridge and would no doubt be keeping the other dogs on their toes and bossing them around.

The vet was called and Netty was sent on her way to the next stage of her life while being held by her Mum and Dad who told her that they loved her so much and that she was a good girl and they thanked her for being their little dog.

Fletcher sat on his bed and as Netty left for her journey, he said quietly "Goodbye Netty."

*Please don't think that once your animals have crossed over that they don't think about you because they do.

They watch over you for quite a while to see that you are OK when you really need them. They hang around you in the form of memories and all the things that they have dug or chewed up.

Or they continue to exist simply through their collar or leash that may be left hanging up on the wall where the owner cannot bear to move it*

At Team Potters House

Pippin was rifling through papers on his desk when his mobile phone rang.

"Hello, Pippin Potter here."

"Hi Pippin, it is Fletcher, can you let everyone know that Netty crossed over to Rainbow Bridge just now."

Pippin went quiet; he always did when there was a crossover to the Bridge. "Right Fletcher, thanks for telling me old chap, I shall make sure everyone knows."

The normally sensible and reserved Pippin began to send the emergency message to all of the gang to notify them that their old friend had gone to Rainbow Bridge.

Pippin had his half rimmed spectacles perched on the end of his pointy snout, he dabbed his eyes with a handkerchief and stared out of the window.

"Are you crying, Pippin?" Bronte asked him.

Turning around to her, Pippin sniffed, "Yes."

"Here, let me." Bronte gently wiped Pippins eyes while ignoring her own tears that left damp patches down her face.

In an unusual display of affection, the two Italian Greyhounds hugged each other tightly for several minutes.

Rainbow Bridge - on arrival

Netty had arrived at Rainbow Bridge; slightly stiff and sore she waited for someone to greet her.

A large white greyhound met her at the gates; he was wearing a beautiful gold soft leather collar and looked so majestic that Netty could not take her eyes off him. "Hi Netty the name is Bowie, pleased to meet you." The greyhound said warmly.

"Hi Bowie, pleased to meet you I am sure." Netty nervously looked around to take in her surroundings.

As if reading her mind Bowie put a large paw on her back, "Don't be nervous, it's not as scary as it looks. Nice things are never scary."

Netty could see dogs in the distance playing, barking, chasing each other and catching a ball or two. There was so much activity going on that she felt a need to join them to see what it was all about. Then remembering that she wasn't able to do that due to old age and poor health, Netty just stared wistfully at the other dogs enjoying themselves.

"So what happens now?" Netty asked Bowie.

"Well, for starters you can go and chase those rabbits we have over there, they are being so naughty they need to be kept in order," Bowie said as one of the rabbits stuck its fingers up at him and wriggled his bottom in an act of defiance.

Netty looked at the rabbits, "I think I am too stiff and sore to chase them, but thank you anyway." She wished that she could, as it looked great fun.

Bowie laughed, "Try it and see, you might surprise yourself."

"What happens if I get lost? I always tend to get lost these days." Netty asked him.

"As I said, just try it" Bowie insisted and used his big snout to give the little dog a nudge in the direction of the naughty rabbits who were busy kicking rabbit droppings everywhere.

Netty slowly started to walk towards the rabbits and to her surprise, she realised that she barely hurt at all and didn't feel so stiff.

She turned around and stared at Bowie who was smiling at her.

"What do I do now?" Netty asked Bowie.

"What do you do? You go and get those rabbits." Bowie barked back and gestured again with his pointy snout.

One step at a time Netty walked closer to the rabbits and with each step that she took she became fitter until she felt no pain at all. She knew exactly where she was and more to the point, she knew that she would never be lost again in the way that an elderly dog can get.

Within five minutes she was chasing those rabbits, and within ten minutes, it was as though she had been there forever.

"Am I there yet Bowie?" Netty turned round and asked him one more time.

"Yes, Netty darling you most certainly are," Bowie replied.

Rainbow Bridge - it is just a nice place to send your pet.

The End

CHAPTER EIGHTEEN

Bitches, Collars and Boy Bands

Pippin Potter was in his study working, you should have gathered by now that Pippin spends a lot of time in his study planning stuff, that's just how he rolls.

Wearing his long dark red housecoat with gold trim and half rimmed spectacles, he sat at his desk working on the Iggy events for the year trying to think about doing something different for his little club.

Picking up his cup of tea he took a mouthful and dabbed his pointy snout with his handkerchief and looked round for Bronte.

"Bronte can you come here a moment as I need to ask you something."

Pippin needed to organise an event that could top all other events but he had run out of ideas himself and this is where Bronte would come in because she often came up with some cool stuff to do.

We won't talk about Bronte's effort at a Moulin Rouge style concert which actually involved Rocco and Brutus dressed up in lacy Basques and doing high kicks and stuff, Madame Gigi is still traumatised by that one.

Bronte was lying on her bed pouring over pop magazines while occasionally picking out bits of dog chow from a bowl but only occasionally as she was watching her weight.

On hearing her name being called, she sighed and got out of her bed to see what Pippin wanted. "Speak quickly Pippin, you have taken me away from my boudoir so it had better be worth it!"

"I am thinking of what we can do for our next Iggy event, do you have any ideas?" Pippin screwed up yet another piece of paper and threw it in the bin.

"Leave it with me, I shall consult with the girls and see what we can come up with," Bronte promised him and went back to her bedroom.

She continued to flick through her magazine, a page titled 'Dogs in Concert' caught her eye and on that page was a picture of five dogs in a successful boy band.

Next to it was a huge write up about what it is like to be famous in the canine world. Bronte flicked the page over to a fitness article.

She quickly turned the page back to the 'Dogs in Concert' article and had a look at it.

"That's it, I've got it!" Jumping off the bed she ran into Pippin's office.

"Pippin, I have the perfect idea for our next Iggy event and you are just going to love it!" Bronte said to Pippin who was making notes on a notepad.

Staring at her over his spectacles, "What is this perfect idea then, tell me about it?"

"This!" Bronte pointed to the article.

"Oh dear," Pippin shook his head.

"The boys can put on a charity concert for the girls, you would only need to sing a couple of songs." Bronte said excitedly, "You could be the lead singer."

"Oh dear, oh dear." Pippin continued to say and took a mouthful of tea to dilute the shock that was hitting his system.

"Oh come on, don't be a spoilsport it will be fun, we can have Brutus in it as well." Bronte pleaded.

"Brutus? He can't sing to save his life!" Pippin spat his English breakfast tea over the keyboard.

"Have some faith in him for goodness sake and I am sure he could do some break dancing or something." Bronte had already made her mind up and there was no persuading her otherwise.

Pippin knew that Brutus's idea of break dancing was lying on the floor and thrashing around as though he was having a fit of some kind.

But still, Brutus was part of the Iggy family and he did look good in leather and would be a good attraction for the girls.

He guessed that it could work; I mean the most unlikely people have managed to form successful boy bands in the past so why couldn't the Iggy lads form a band of their own?

Pippin agreed, "Right, you are on! Let's do a charity Dogs in Concert type thing and any money we make can go to the dogs' home."

"You will all need professional coaching, so we will have to think of someone suitable because Brutus is going to need all the help he can get," Bronte said.

"That's easy, there is only one dog I know that has the class to carry that task off," Pippin replied.

"Eugeen the Angry Afghan!" They both said at the same time and laughed.

Eugeen the angry Afghan whom you have all met earlier in the book, is a large, black, majestic and grumpy Afghan hound prone to dramatic outbursts towards any dogs that dare walk too close to him.

He is flamboyant, 'camp' and draws attention wherever he goes. If anyone could coach the new doggy boy band it is Eugeen; I mean that dog could even teach me how to sing and dance I am sure.

"Dogs in Concert it is then." Bronte cheered and high-fived Pippin who felt quite proud as he did it because 'high-fiving' always made him feel rebellious, a bit like flipping the finger behind the back of your science teacher.

Picking up her phone from the table, Bronte typed up a group text to the girls in the club 'You will never guess what the Iggy club is going to do...'

Pippin waited until Bronte had left the room and checked out his reflection in the mirror.

Sucking in his waist, he stood in various poses and wondered if he could actually learn to sing and dance in time for the concert.

He would also have to cast others for the band and that could cause some arguments or jealousy but there was no point in worrying about that yet.

Pippin winked at his reflection and clicked his paws. He could do this, he could do it because it was for charity and he could do it because deep down inside he knew that it would be fun.

He walked over to his computer and began composing an email to the boys in the group. Not knowing how to word it or what to say, he wrote, 'Meeting at mine tomorrow, bring your bones and your attitude but no girls allowed'.

Then laughing at his own bravery, he hit 'send' before his sensible side could stop him.

The next day

The Iggies rocked up at Pippin's in high spirits with each of them wondering what on earth could be so urgent for such an impromptu meeting, not to mention the cryptic message Pippin had sent them.

"I hope it is not a boot-camp or something equally awful." Rocco sighed to Kaya.

Kaya said nothing but inwardly thought that if it were going to be a boot camp then he would pretend to break at least two of his legs in order to get out of it.

Fat Harry remained quiet. He was wondering why the girls were not invited to this as they always did everything as a group so this was odd. But before he got a chance to voice his concerns, the doorbell rang with more visitors.

"That will be the door!" Shelby shouted to nobody in particular and debated whether or not to answer it. After a few seconds he decided to do the guard dog thing and bark instead.

Chewy shuffled to the door where he could see Brutus and Rocky's heads peering through the glass. This pleased him immensely because he always had fun when he was with Brutus. He jumped onto a chair and gripped the door handle and wriggled his bum a few times to open the door for them.

"Hi guys, don't suppose you know what this is all about, do you?" Chewy asked them.

Rocky shook his head and said that he knew nothing and that he hoped it wasn't too energetic as he was actually disabled and that would just be cruel.

Rocky is kind of on a par with Rocco the Iggy because while Rocco has Tourette's and invisible friends to fight with, Rocky has his grump on with most real life dogs and a few pretend ones too.

Rocco was feeling quite twitchy himself and on the verge of starting a fight with an invisible dog that was taunting him and making him feel inadequate. Picking up on Rocco's anger signals, Pippin knew that he had to get the announcement underway to calm them all down.

Standing up on his chair Pippin did a loud cough "Excuse me everyone, I guess you are all wondering why you are here?" Carlos, Deejay, Rocco, Fat Harry, Chewy, Brutus, Rocky, Dash, Giovanni and Shelby all sat around the living room hanging on to Pippin's every word.

"Come on old chap, get on with it!" Shelby heckled, a few of the others barked in agreement and for a moment it looked as though it might get out of hand.

"I can't imagine why they want me here," Rocky whispered to Brutus.

"Nor can I, you hate everyone and you are a cripple," Brutus replied truthfully causing Rocco to snort with laughter.

"He's got your number Rocky, Brutus knows you too well!" Rocco sniggered.

"That is not funny, that is SO not funny." Rocky glared at his brother and looked boot-faced at everyone else to gain sympathy.

He should walk out now while he still had his dignity but then he remembered that his hips were sore and he probably couldn't if he tried. So he sat there with his lips pursed together in his regulation 'cats bum' shape and purposely shuffled a few inches away from Brutus just to prove his point.

Regulation cats bum is where someone purses their lips tightly like a cats anus, this is usually done in disapproval. It is not a flattering pose so if you are prone to doing the 'RCB - Regulation Cats Bum' expression, watch out because it looks quite ridiculous and who wants a mouth like a bum?

"Are you all listening?" Pippin clapped his paws together at the excited chattering Iggies, "Hello! Can you boys all stop gossiping please?"

"Gossip? Who is he calling a gossip?" Chewy whispered to Kaya and by the time Kaya thought of a suitable reply, his teeth had stuck to his lips again and he couldn't talk.

Slowly they all looked up at Pippin; keen to hear what he had to say. Satisfied that he had gotten their attention, Pippin began to tell him the news and secretly hoped that they would find it as exciting as he did.

"I have finalised the idea for the Iggy event of the year and without further ado I am excited to tell you that I shall be selecting some of you for a charity boy band and we will be holding a concert to raise money for the dogs' home."

"Did he just say boy band?" Rocco mouthed to Brutus.

"I think so." Brutus nodded and tilted his head to try to hear better, because there is nothing like tilting your head to make a difference. A bit like turning down the radio in your car so you don't miss your turning.

"Who is going to be in this boy band?" Chewie barked.

Ignoring him Pippin carried on speaking, "Well, I have been busy gathering information on successful boy bands and have figured that we will be doing two cover songs from the 80s." Pippin went to his desk and turned on his CD player to start playing the songs that he had chosen.

"I didn't know they had music in Victorian times?" Chewie said to Rocky who explained to him that every era had its own music of some sort and this was certainly not Victorian music.

"Yes, but who is going to be in it?" Shelby asked Pippin.

"Myself, Brutus, Rocco, Chewy, Kaya, Fat Harry and Rocky" Pippin reeled off the names.

"Did he just say our names?" Kaya asked Rocco.

Rocco replied that yes he had certainly heard their names mentioned but not to get too excited in case they had heard it wrong.

Fat Harry was already dreaming of success, hot bitches and steaks and not necessarily in that order. Kaya, Chewy and Brutus sat there looking stunned wondering if they could pull it off.

Only Rocky didn't say anything and that was because he thought that Pippin had made a mistake in choosing him. Because who in their right mind would want a disabled Kelpie in their band slowing things down and ruining their reputation as pop stars?

"Are you sure Pippin, that you want me in the band?" Rocky frowned.

Pippin knew that the grumpy old kelpie rarely got to do as much as the other dogs because of his bad hips. Yes, he was absolutely sure he had made the right decision.

"Yes, Rocky I am quite sure and I have every faith in you that you can do it as well."

Rocky stood up straight and even though his hips were sore, he slowly walked over to Pippin and shook his paw and gave him a 'man-hug'.

A man hug is the kind of hugs guys give to one another that have significant meaning yet have to be seen to be 'cool' so nobody gets embarrassed

"Don't mention it old chap, don't mention it." Pippin patted Rocky on the back and did a loud cough to distract him from getting emotional.

Rocky sat back down next to Brutus, "Sorry for not believing in you earlier Rocky, you are going to make a great pop star."

"Even though I have bad hips?" Rocky gave an embarrassed smile.

"That makes you even more of a star in my opinion." Brutus shrugged.

Rocky wiped his eyes and tried not to cry, not because he was nervous, but because he was so proud to be included.

Sometimes you have to persist with grumpy people because once you get past 'the grump', there is usually a great personality waiting to get out which is the case with Rocky and many dogs like him.

Rocco raised his paw to get Pippin's attention, "So what are we going to call ourselves then?"

"How about Bones of Attitude?" Fat Harry suggested.

"That is so lame, oh my god we can do better than that surely?" Rocco scorned at the idea.

Pippin took a sip of his coffee, "The name has already been decided, and we are going to call ourselves The Breeder Boyz, with a Z of course."

Looking more than a little proud of himself he stared at the others to take in the admiring looks of most of the Iggies, well I say most because Giovanni was looking pretty disgusted.

"Problem Giovanni?" Pippin asked him.

Giovanni was already prepared with his answer, "None of you have testicles, and you will look silly calling yourselves that when you don't have any balls of your own."

To prove his point, Giovanni held up a dog magazine with a photo of an Iggie with his testicles hanging down like Christmas doorbells.

Pippin looked at Brutus and Rocco and told them that they could be in charge of the testicle situation, leaving Brutus wondering how could they magic up some testicles in time.

"Don't worry Brutus, I have the most awesome idea." Rocco wagged his tail and nipped Brutus on his hind leg.

Rocky who as you know is Mr Respectable, shook his head, "I don't even want to know what they are planning, but I hope that I am not involved."

Chewy, Kaya and Fat Harry agreed but knew once Rocco had an idea, it was usually something 'out there' and secondly, as the band was called 'The Breeder Boyz,' then this idea would have to involve all of them including Rocky.

As they all looked at one another, Chewy forced a smile and said, "How bad can it be?"

Rocky didn't reply, but he did look up to the sky and say a quick prayer for his reputation and his sanity.

"Come on Brutus, let's have a testicle meeting." Rocco barked.

"What is a testicle meeting?" Brutus scratched his head and looked puzzled.

"It's a meeting about testicles, now come on as we have no time to lose." and in one swift movement Rocco leapt up onto Brutus's back, pointed to the direction of the bedrooms and yelled "Take me there big boy!" As Brutus trotted off with Rocco gripping on for dear life while shouting "Not so fast, you are banging my willy!"

"I wonder what they are planning?" Rocky asked Chewy.

Chewy flicked his tail a few times, which he always did when he was agitated, "I don't know but no doubt we shall find out, I hope it is nothing rude though."

As the familiar sounds of Brutus and Rocco snorting with laughter could be heard from the other room. Pippin shook his head and sighed, "God help us."

"Check this out guys, you can call me Super Balls!" Brutus appeared in the living room and stood there with a couple of oranges dangling in an orange netting bag.

"Oh my god, that is....." Fletcher struggled and failed to find the right words.

"Bloody genius I reckon" Carlos nodded.

"But how on earth, where on earth, just how?" Fletcher stuttered.

Brutus said nothing but was looking quite pleased as he walked like a cowboy towards the boys to show them how it worked.

"Oranges? Really?" Chewy rubbed his eyes several times as if hoping to wake up from the nightmare.

"What do you reckon Rocky?" Brutus said proudly to the little black kelpie.

Rocky looked at Brutus and Rocco; removing his kelpie spectacles and wiping them on a handkerchief, he glanced between his legs and then looked at Brutus's oranges with a pained expression on his face. "I have no words."

"It's OK Rocky, don't look my friend, just don't look." Chewy soothed, and covered Rocky's eyes with his paws to hide the trauma and shock of it all.

"Of course Pippin as the lead singer will have something far superior to these," Brutus told them.

"Like what?" Shelby asked, he was still feeling sensitive over the loss of his own testicles and thought it was a crying shame that he didn't sell them on eBay as he would have gotten a fortune for them.

"Can't tell you, it's meant to be a secret," Brutus said while trying to juggle the oranges in his paws and then yelped because one hit him in the eye. "But you are going to be seriously impressed." He quickly walked away before the Iggies could grill him for further information.

Pippin jumped on to the table and barked to shut everyone up, "Right everyone, I declare this meeting over. Bronte will be back home soon and we haven't even eaten yet.

"We shall meet up again in two days' time at the venue and in the meantime I shall email you with a list of what needs to be done and by whom."

"Hold on, where is the venue? You haven't told us?" Rocky questioned Pippin.

"Ah yes, the venue, it is going to be held at the local obedience hall.

"I have managed to secure that this morning, aren't we lucky!" Pippin said with rather too much enthusiasm, as he knew the Iggies would be scared in case it involved awful stuff like obedience.

But before they had a chance to complain, Pippin was ushering them out of the house as he had to tidy up his toys before Bronte got back from her night with the girls. She hated mess and would not be happy if his squeaky toys and mobile phones were lying around cluttering the place up.

"How exciting!" Fat Harry said as the Iggy gang left Pippin's house.

"Except for the fact that none of us can dance." Rocky piped up.

"Oh Pippin will have that covered, Pippin has everything covered." Shelby barked and despite their reservations, the others agreed with him because they knew he was right. Pippin could organise the world if he was given the opportunity.

Two days later at the big meeting

Rocky, Brutus and Bronte had turned up at the obedience hall where Shelby, Rocco, Giovanni and Fat Harry were huddled around a parking space with a pot of blue paint while Pippin stood over them overseeing everything.

"Shelby you are getting it all wonky!" Pippin snapped as Shelby tried to paint something on the ground.

"Do we really need this, I mean really?" Fat Harry yawned. Bored by the whole thing he wondered if it was lunchtime; as you all know, Fat Harry's entire life revolves around food.

"Rocky is my mate and I like to do my bit for the disabled," Pippin replied with a martyred look.

"Do what for the disabled?" Rocky said suspiciously as he walked up behind them.

"Oh hello Rocky, we have a surprise for you." Rocco grinned.

"Rocky! You are here at last! How are you old chap?" Pippin rushed forward to meet his kelpie friend.

"What in the name of God is that?" Rocky asked looking horrified. For there in front of him was a crude attempt at drawing a blue disabled parking bay for kelpies. But instead of a wheelchair symbol like the standard human one, there was a bright blue circle with the word 'Rocky' with the 'C' written back to front in the middle of the circle.

"Don't worry about the shape, I mean while it isn't a perfect parking spot, it will do for you" Shelby tried to reason with him.

"Oh dear" Bronte sighed, "Pippin what were you thinking?"

Rocco who had been polite for so long was now close to meltdown as Pippin hadn't let him draw a penis in the parking space, and had started to grumble to his invisible friends about not being allowed to have any fun.

"You are SO ungrateful Rocky, I mean there are many dogs that would be happy to have a disabled spot reserved just for them."

"I don't even have a wheelchair so it is of no use to me." Rocky said looking hurt, "Besides I only have hip dysplasia so I am not that disabled."

"That's true, he doesn't have a wheelchair" Bronte tried to calm the situation and be the voice of reason.

"But you are disabled Rocky, Mum said that you fell over in the garden while trying to take a shit the other day." Brutus blurted out.

"Oh don't exaggerate; I merely over balanced that was all." Rocky snapped, clearly embarrassed and annoyed that Brutus had dobbed him in.

"Well, about the wheelchair..." Pippin struggled to find the right words just as Shelby came from behind the corner pushing a tatty wheelchair with a red tartan cover on the back. In the wheelchair was Giovanni who was barking and humming the inspirational music used to play at sports events.

"What do you think?" Pippin looked at Rocky, "It will scrub up nicely with a bit of leather and gold studs."

Rocky took off his round spectacles and rubbed his eyes, pursing his lips tightly all he could say was "Please God tell me I am dreaming. Pippin, please tell me that this is a joke!"

"He likes it really, I can just tell," Brutus whispered to Giovanni who did a thumbs-up sign back to him.

"What do you think? Do you like it, isn't it fabulous?" Giovanni asked Rocky who was looking as though he might combust.

I won't tell you what Rocky said, as it was very rude. But as the senior kelpie hobbled off with Bronte and Brutus, you could hear him making suggestions as to where to put the tartan wheelchair and disabled parking space and to give you a hint, the word used was 'arse'.

"Do you think he likes it?" Pippin asked Rocco.

Rocco nodded a couple of times, "Loves it, totally loves it, Rocky is gonna rock that wheelchair!"

"Right then that's enough, everyone back inside, we need to plan these rehearsals."

Pippin picked up his clipboard and five mobile phones and went back inside. Leaving Giovanni to pick up the painting gear, while Chewy scuttled behind him complaining about some paint that had gotten stuck to the fur on his bum.

Back inside

The Iggies sat at the table checking all of their social media accounts. Rocco had already tagged himself at the venue and updated his status using the hash tag '#TheLyfeofaPopstar'.

"Can you all pay attention please and that includes you Rocco, you can do your social media updates afterwards." Pippin glared at him.

"Just doing my bit to raise media awareness, you are SO ungrateful Pippin!" Rocco looked offended. He had changed his profile photo and had done one of those selfies where you try to look sexy by winking at the camera. Only instead of looking sexy, he looked like he had a foreign body in his eye instead.

"We all must learn to sing, dance and play our part and for that we need an instructor, someone that knows how to prance and show off and someone that has charisma", said Pippin while making notes.

Fat Harry looked confused, "But who do we know who can do that?"

"Eugeen the Angry Afghan that's who, he is the perfect dog for the job," Pippin said quickly before anyone else could question him.

"But what can Eugeen teach us that one of our own can't?" Rocco asked.

The last time they saw Eugeen was when Pippin and Vader were getting ballroom dancing lessons from him and there were lots of tight pants involved and hip wriggling.

"Everything my friend, Eugeen can teach us everything." Pippin waved his paws dismissively.

"We start rehearsals first thing in the morning so please bring your dancing shoes.

"If you could please pay attention, I shall now tell you what part each of you will be playing in the band.

"Brutus and I will be singers. Fat Harry and Chewy are dancers and backing singers, Rocco is on the drums, Kaya plays the mouth organ with his teeth and Rocky is on the keyboards and will be expected to do cheeky manoeuvres across the stage."

"Cheeky manoeuvres across the stage? Are you kidding me?" Rocky interrupted him.

"No old chap and furthermore I think you will be jolly good at it." Pippin beamed at Rocky.

"Well, I am flattered at your confidence in me but Pippin, just one thing?" Rocky asked him.

"What's that Rocky?" Pippin waited for Rocky's response.

"No wheelchair," Rocky said as firmly as he possibly could and then added "Absolutely NO wheelchair." but what he didn't see was the boys doing the thumbs-up gesture behind his back.

Rehearsals

Obviously, as any successful boy band will tell you, rehearsals are next to godliness, and if you want to get those dance moves on-point, then you have to practice. I mean, all the top boy bands didn't get to where they are today without practising their dance moves I am sure.

Pippin, Brutus, Kaya, Fat Harry, Rocky, and Rocco were in Pippin's living room for rehearsals. The furniture had been pushed back or moved to make space for dancing (and wheelchairs), and all breakable ornaments had been put on the kitchen counter.

The girls had gone round to Gigi's house for some wine and dog chow and to pick out their clothes for what they were going to wear at the concert.

Brutus had been up late the night before getting quite distressed because he couldn't find his 'dancing shoes' and it took a great deal of explanation from Pippin to get him to understand that 'dancing shoes' was an expression and not actual footwear.

Eugeen the angry Afghan had now been established as the official choreographer and singing teacher. Having done ballroom dancing in the past, he was the obvious choice to help them plus he could play the piano, as well so he was a good all-rounder to show them the ropes.

He had rocked up at Pippin's wearing his red satin flared pants with studs down the sides and a black satin vest and he looked every inch the rock star.

Eugeen not only wriggled when he walked but was able to make everyone want to copy him as well because he made his famous wriggle 'the new black'. Rocco did point out that Eugeen walked as though he had a toffee stuffed up his bum but we can't mention that as Eugeen is still upset by that particular comment.

"Come on boys and girls, let's get this show on the road!" Eugeen yelled in his camp voice, which he had hammed up for effect. His long glossy black fur, which looked like something out of a shampoo advert, gave off wafts of cologne with each movement.

The Iggies were too busy trying to shout over each other to listen to him and were oblivious to the large black dog that was fast losing his patience with them.

Eugeen tried to silence the group by clapping his fluffy paws on the table. Their high pitched voices were all trying to out-talk one another as they decided who would make the best sex symbol of the band and what they would be wearing for their big night.

"Helloooooooo! Are you lot going to listen to me or do I have to squirt the lot of you with water?" Then dipping his paws in a bowl of water, he flicked it over the excited Iggies to shut them up.

"I say that was bloody rude! You ought to know that small dogs like us actually melt when we get wet! Pippin, Eugeen has just assaulted us with water!" Chewy said to Pippin while dabbing his fur with a tea towel.

Pippin ignored him, leaving Chewy mumbling something to Rocco about how dangerously unpleasant water can be to tiny dogs, next to bull ants of course and any self-respecting Australian dog knows what bastards they can be.

"You will be singing a couple of songs that Pippin and I have personally chosen for you." Eugeen started to say before Fat Harry cut him off with questions.

"Are they good songs Eugeen, will they make us sound like superstars?" Fat Harry interrupted.

Eugeen looked at his team and worked his eyes around the room. Brutus with his baggy pants on with poo stains on the back. Then there was Rocky who walked like he was wearing callipers.

Fat Harry who was bursting out of his pants and his gravy stained T-shirt strained over his huge belly. Chewy who looked permanently insulted by life, and Rocco who swore like he breathed and fought with invisible friends.

Kaya's top lip seemed to be permanently stuck to his upper teeth and Pippin who looked like a choirboy going through a rebellious phase.

This was going to be a huge challenge and he certainly had his work cut out for him. Taking a deep breath Eugeen replied tactfully "You are all going to be rock stars."

"Just like Dogstar Williams?" Pippin asked hopefully. (Dogstar Williams is a famous canine pop singer that most dogs hero worship)

"Just like Dogstar Williams." Eugeen nodded.

What nobody realised was that even Eugeen himself wasn't sure if he could pull this one off, but he couldn't let the boys know that, as they were depending on him and Eugeen did not 'do' failure.

Would he be the one to turn them into rock stars and would the group be ready and prepared in time for the concert? Who knows but as I have just said, the word 'failure' is not in his vocabulary.

Inside the concert hall

It was the night of the concert; the boys were inside getting ready and in high spirits. Eugeen was working the crowds like a drag queen by periodically walking on stage to check what was going on and raising a cheer each time he did it.

The atmosphere was that of excitement and anticipation as the Iggies impatiently waited for the concert to start. The girls were busy applying their make up and touching up their collars for the tenth time in an hour and asking each other if they looked good enough.

Georgina was wearing a ballet skirt, with purple gaudy looking stockings, a pair of steel toe capped boots, a white vest, leather studded wrist bracelets and an oversized chunky studded collar around her neck.

"I am making a fashion statement," Georgina said confidently as Nica eyed her up and down as though she had grown horns on her head.

"You are making people stare," Nica hissed back at her, "have you not heard of being respectable?"

Georgina didn't care though, she enjoyed being different and this concert was the perfect place to do it. There was no way she would be stripping her collar off to throw at any boy band.

"Respectable Schmectable!" Georgina barked back at Nica who pulled such a face of disapproval that Gigi had to tell her to stop before the wind changed direction and it would remain on her face forever. That's what my Mum used to say to me when I poked my tongue out at my sister, it never did though so I reckon Mum had it wrong.

Bronte was super excited, as she knew that her brother was in the band. She never imagined that he would be brave enough to participate in such a thing so you can imagine what a big thing this was for all concerned.

Eugeen was dressed up in tight purple satin flared pants and a tight black vest with 'Bitches, Bones and my Mum' on the front of his top. He was quite a showstopper, as he trotted around the hall while telling the odd invisible dog to stop pissing on his stage.

The other dogs hadn't seen anything quite so glamorous since Shimmer the French poodle was in town, wearing a diamond collar and speaking in a French accent while smoking French cigarettes.

"Eugeen! What's occurring? Where are the boys? Tell me everything!" Bronte launched herself at Eugeen after all Pippin was her brother and she had the right to know.

"Do you want the answer to that Bronte?" Eugeen flicked his ears back and popped a mint into his mouth.

"What's that?" Bronte leaned forward and tried to snatch one of his long black hairs as a souvenir.

"Patience-pie and lots of it", Eugeen affectionately patted Bronte on her bottom. He walked off leaving her blushing and wondering where she could buy patience-pie from and if it contained any calories.

"They are taking ages, what on earth are they doing? Surely they must be ready now." Olivia whispered to Zara.

Zara was putting on another layer of mascara and spraying herself with so much perfume that poor Dash got some as well and started coughing.

"It's all going to kick off in a minute if Eugeen doesn't get the band on stage," Carlos said to Deejay.

He was right, as some of the Iggies had started to stamp their little feet on the floor just like people do at concerts. Except for a 5kg Iggy, it doesn't have much impact so they had started to bark as well and make wolf noises or as Brutus calls it, 'singing the song of their people'.

"These girls are behaving like animals." Deejay shook his head at the sight of the female

Iggies squealing because they were so hyped up and excited.

"They are animals," Carlos replied leaving Deejay looking hurt and confused because all these years he thought that all Iggies were human.

Behind the scenes

The fake testicles had been securely fastened behind the dog's tails. Rocco, Chewy, Rocky, Kaya and Fat Harry were wearing their tangerines inside the stretchy-netted bag tied with a black silk ribbon and elastic band behind their tails. Brutus being such a big boy had two large oranges in his bag and Pippin was somewhat more glamorous and had a pair of plums with some glitter on them.

Although Brutus and Rocco had organised the fake testicles and had tried to find matching tangerines for all the band members, poor old Fat Harry had drawn the short straw and had one small tangerine and one large orange which made him look lopsided.

"I look like I have some kind of testicle problem, perhaps I should go and see the doctor just to be safe. What do you think Eugeen?" Harry strained his head round to check on his oranges, which did look quite ridiculous.

"Darling, you don't have testicles, these are just oranges my sweetie so please stop panicking." Eugeen laughed.

Harry still wasn't happy and muttered something about how one can never be too careful when it comes to the health of one's testicles whether they are real or fake.

The boys were all wearing tight black jeans, black leather jackets and black T-shirts all individually personalised.

Pippin was trying to distract himself by practising holding his belly in because his black jeans were obscenely tight. His T-shirt had 'Bitches, Bones and Balls' on the front and he wore a large gold chain around his neck with a diamond encrusted mobile phone pendant.

Kaya wasn't talking to anyone because his lips had stuck to his teeth and he needed Brutus to peel them down for him. His T-shirt read 'Bitches, Bones and Teeth' and because Eugeen could only get him some whippet jeans, they were obviously far too long for him and he had to roll them up at the ankles.

Rocco looked pretty good in his outfit; his T shirt read 'Bitches, Bones and Bollocks' on the front while Chewy's T shirt had 'Boys, Bones and bums' which summed Chewy up perfectly.

Because of Chewy's long fur, he had to have black baggy jeans instead of tight ones, which he was pleased about, as you all know Chewy, he likes to stand out from the crowd.

Rocco nearly caused a rumpus with Chewy when he said with the amount of Chewy's fur stuffed into his baggy jeans, he looked as though he had shit himself but Pippin told him to keep that opinion to himself.

Rocky was firmly established in his wheelchair, you know the wheelchair that he had point blank refused to entertain using? Eugeen and the other boys had jazzed up the chair and the seating had been changed for leather covering.

The chair had gold studs down the back in the shape of a kelpie's head and around the edges of the wheels was fluorescent stickers that reflected in the dark. It did look rather spangly if I do say so myself but the best part was a couple of fireworks strapped to each side.

"You OK Rocky, ready to roll?" Eugeen bent down to straighten Rocky's collar in a way that your Mum would straighten out your school tie.

Rocky nodded curtly and said that yes, he was just fine but had serious doubts about the 'Geek Chic' kind of image.

Wearing his leather jacket and tight kelpie jeans, his T-shirt had 'Bitches, bones and tennis balls' on the front. His round spectacles and thick leather studded collar with a sheep pendant clipped on it completed the image.

"Do I really need to have my legs like this?" Rocky argued. His legs had been carefully splayed out to give the impression that he was more disabled than he actually was.

"It gets the sympathy votes my friend, you win points for hip dysplasia as well so let's run with it shall we?" Eugeen tried to reason with him,

"Oh my god did you see what I did there? Let's run with it, get it?" he giggled at Rocky, "God I am funny when I want to be, I do make myself laugh you know!"

"Glad you find my bad hips so amusing" Rocky growled, "But I am warning you, after this concert has finished I am out of this wheelchair, do I make myself clear?"

"Crystal clear darling," Eugeen promised and quickly ran off to check on the others before Rocky could wind himself up further.

"Kaya my love, please lubricate your teeth because you look like a shark." Eugeen could be heard shouting at Kaya.

With his lip stuck firmly to his gums, Kaya spoke with a pronounced 'lisp'. "Thath not very polite ith it?" Kaya said to Fat Harry; he wasn't really listening though.

Fat Harry's button had popped open on his jeans and he had to call on the help of Brutus to assist. "Breathe in Harry!" Brutus panted as he tried to force the button to do up.

"I am trying!" Fat Harry gasped, "I can't think why they won't button up, I have barely been eating, starving myself in fact."

"What about those 12 burgers you stole off the BBQ yesterday not to mention the buns that went with them?" Brutus reminded him.

"That was just a snack and I didn't eat for at least an hour afterwards. Hold on a minute, something is happening." Fat Harry stopped talking and went rigid and did the most enormous fart. "That's better, let's try again,"

"How do I look Brutus?" He asked in a strained voice. The button on his jeans was now done up and his belly was hanging over the waistband. His T-shirt, which was obscenely tight, had 'Bitches, Bones and Starvation' on the front, he looked at Brutus, eagerly awaiting his opinion.

Brutus looked at Fat Harry for a few minutes, "Hold on a second,"

Brutus tidied up Harry's ears, which were sticking out like the handles of a bicycle. He pulled out a tissue from his pocket and wet it with some drool and proceeded to wipe some tomato sauce off Harry's face. It was a sweet moment between the two boys that really was quite magical.

"Let me look at you now," Brutus took a step back to get a better view of Fat Harry, "Bloody marvellous, you my friend are rocking it," Brutus said firmly and handed him his leather jacket.

Because in Brutus's eyes Harry did look marvellous and that is what friendship is all about, seeing the good in people and telling them so.

"Thanks, Brutus, you look pretty good yourself mate," Harry said gratefully and then walked off like a penguin because his jeans were too tight.

Brutus was dressed up in his tight black jeans, tight black T-shirt with 'Bitches, Bones and Tony Abbott' on the front and a black leather jacket.

His ears had been sprayed with hair spray to make them permanently erect and he was wearing a thick studded leather collar with a silver tag on it in the shape of a bone. He actually looked pretty good and for once his size went in his favour.

But Brutus was fractious and unsettled; this was the biggest event in his life and he was terrified. You all know how bad his dyslexia gets when he is nervous and his tendency to join 'The Diarrhoea Brothers' at inappropriate times.

"I need to go for a poo," Brutus said to Chewy. Wrinkling his nose in disgust, Chewy moved away from Brutus to put some distance between them. Brutus was already doing the type of farts you do before you have a poo that makes everyone hold their nose and accuse you of soiling yourself.

"Excuse me Eugeen, I need to do a poo," Brutus shouted at the top of his voice while holding his front paw in the air to get Eugeen's attention. This outburst was followed by a series of farts, which were getting dangerously closer together and burning the nostrils of all in the vicinity.

"Do you have to announce it to the whole world?" A mortified Pippin screwed his face up.

"My Mum always asks me if I need to do a poo before we go out." Brutus tried to explain.

"Yes, that's as may be, but we don't need to know that you need to do a poo Brutus." Pippin reprimanded him, "Can't you hold it?"

Brutus blushed and clenched his bottom cheeks together and hoped that he wouldn't let everyone down by shitting himself. Apart from being embarrassing, there wasn't much room in his trousers to accommodate it, and if it went through his netting bag containing the oranges then it would not end well.

Spotting the anxiety on Brutus's face and noticing that his bottom lip was quivering, Pippin knew from experience that Brutus would indeed end up soiling himself on stage. He also knew that there was not enough time to put him outside to do it either.

He looked around to see what he could use for Brutus to go to the toilet in. Brutus was farting like a champion and the stench was getting worse and he was getting more distressed and repeatedly mouthing the words 'I need a poo'.

Pippin spotted a large handbag next to an elderly poodle that was sitting by the edge of the stage. The poodle was oblivious to Pippin and was busy cleaning her spectacles and eating mints (what is it with old people and eating mints?)

Making sure the poodle wasn't looking, he grabbed the handbag and threw it at Brutus. He hissed "You will have to do it in that, it's a good size so your bum should fit now hurry up!"

Brutus didn't need telling twice and pulled his jeans down while Pippin quickly pulled a curtain around him and stood there with his arms folded, whistling and pretending to look at the ceiling cracks.

"I sincerely hope that you haven't shit in your testicle bag, have you finished yet? We are on stage any minute now, you must hurry up!"

Then hearing a loud thud as the turd hit the bottom of the handbag, Pippin added "Jesus Christ is that you Brutus? What on earth have you eaten?"

"That's better, I feel so much lighter, thanks, Pippin." Brutus emerged from behind the curtain still doing up his jeans. "Can you organise my ball bag please and check they are in order?"

Pippin did a quick check on the netted bag tied to Brutus's tail and quickly re-organised the 'testicles'.

"Thanks' Pippin, you are a star," and handed Pippin the handbag full of his poo which Pippin nearly dropped due to the weight of it.

He didn't get the chance to say anything else as Eugeen was calling them on stage so Pippin hurriedly zipped the bag up and kicked it back next to the poodle that was later seen dragging her handbag along the ground muttering loudly about how heavy her bag was.

"Everyone, take your places on the stage, Brutus you can help Rocky get into position.

"Pippin, Chewy, Kaya, Rocco and Fat Harry, you all know where you have to be so get to it and don't forget to make sure your testicle bags are in place!" Eugeen barked and waved dramatically with his long hairy legs to demonstrate where they should all go.

Poor Fat Harry with one orange and one tangerine looked very off balance but there was nothing anyone could do now because there was no time.

The boys took their places from behind the curtains - Chewy on the drums, Kaya with his mouth organ, Fat Harry and Rocco as dancers/ backing singers and Brutus and Pippin as lead singers.

Only one dog was missing, in their excitement they had forgotten to wheel Rocky out in his wheelchair and the little black kelpie was sitting at the side of the stage in his chair like a spare part looking utterly panic stricken.

"Pssst! You forgot about Rocky!" Pippin hissed at Brutus who mouthed the words "Oh shit."

"You can't just leave me here like a lemon!" Rocky said helplessly, but the boys on the stage couldn't hear him and were too wrapped up in their own nerves to even notice.

"Ladies and gentlemen, especially the ladies!" Eugeen announced and winked at Zara.

"Oooh that Eugeen is quite dashing I must say," Zara said to Olivia. Olivia nodded and gave Bronte a sharp poke in the ribs so that she could also appreciate the handsome Afghan in all of his furry glory of flamboyance and glamour.

"I would like to present to you our very own home grown boy band. Perth's next biggest thing and dogs that our ladies would remove their collars for, The Breeder Boyz!" Eugeen thrust his front legs into the air to encourage the audience to clap.

From behind the scenes Vader the boxer had been instructed to play a recording of girls screaming and sobbing at a boy band concert, just to give the illusion of a good crowd. But having mixed up the recordings, Vader had put on the Australian National Anthem on instead.

"Nothing wrong with a bit of patriotism I guess" Nica said to Zara who mumbled something about 'never heard this song before and who sings it?'

The curtains slowly started to open as brothers Deejay and Carlos tugged on them from each end, they were pretty heavy for two little Iggies to open but the boys did a good job all things considered.

Eugeen had noticed that poor old Rocky had been left behind in his wheelchair and if he weren't moved soon then it would be a disaster. Eugeen signalled to Vader who stood in the corner pretending that the Australian National Anthem was part of the show and was waving his paws encouragingly at the bewildered audience to try to get them to clap.

"Get the kelpie out now!" Eugeen nodded towards the trembling and embarrassed Rocky who was sitting in his wheelchair. His two oranges (testicles) in the bag were now the wrong way round and resting on his tummy like a bag of shopping.

"What the hell are you doing?" Rocky growled at Vader who had snuck on stage behind the curtains and was attempting to lift the brakes off the wheelchair.

"Saving your bacon, that's what I am doing" Vader replied in a grim voice and then pulled some matches from his pocket, he quickly lit the fireworks on Rocky's chair. Then using every ounce of his strength, he pushed Rocky across the stage so that he shot out like a rocket just in time for the curtain to fully open.

Thankfully all the audience saw was Rocky whizzing past at great speed and luckily managing to stop right in the middle next to Pippin Potter, just as the two fireworks went off and scorched his eyebrows into the bargain.

The audience thought it was part of the act and the girls screamed with excitement and started barking.

"Ooooh, that was clever, wasn't that clever Zara, did you see the fireworks?" Nica gasped as Rocky flew across the stage with smoke coming out from each side of his chair.

Their moment had finally arrived, they had all worked so hard for this night and the Iggy girls had been not so patiently waiting to see their boys as superstars.

Dressed in tight jeans, T-shirts and leather jackets with their testicle bags tied at the base of their tails, the boys looked every inch the pop stars that they were meant to be.

Pippin and Brutus stood in the middle of the stage, wearing their headset microphones to enable them to be heard; all they had to do was remember their lyrics.

Brutus kept looking down to check his paws because unbeknown to anyone else, Eugeen had told him to write, 'And I love my Mum' on one paw and 'Poo on my bum' on the other in case he forgot his lyrics, because Eugeen had figured that saying anything was better than nothing.

Pippin had been up the entire night worrying about his impending performance, and while he had an excellent memory for stuff like that, he was still scared and felt as though he could burst into tears at any given moment.

To calm Pippin down Eugeen had given him a leather wrist band with studs on it so when Pippin got scared, he could press the studs on the wrist band to bring him back to reality. Please don't tell Pippin I told you that, as he is still embarrassed about it.

Fat Harry, Chewy, Kaya and Rocco don't usually suffer with their nerves but in the event that they did, they were told to imagine a bowl full of treats to keep their focus.

As for Rocky, well he had perhaps the biggest part because he had to adapt to a wheelchair, become a doggy sexy symbol as well as play the keyboards with one paw and have a good poker face (girls love that so I hear).

"Pippin?" Brutus whispered to Pip who was doing a quick last minute fiddle of his plums.

"Yes Brutus?" Pippin replied.

"I am scared" Brutus whimpered but never got the chance to say anything else as the backing music had started for the first song. This was their moment and there was no going back.

The boys sing their first song 'Bones larger than Life' - sung by the (fictitious) doggy boy band 'Backstreet Hound Dogs'

This is where you will need to download some good old fashion 80s boy band tunes and play them now. Put on your headphones and imagine the boys on stage doing their stuff, feel free to sing along to offer your support

"Oh my god, I LOVE the Backstreet Hound Dogs, Nica do you remember them? I TOTALLY remember them!" Zara barked in Nica's ear.

Nica brought her back to reality by telling Zara that she wasn't actually alive when the Backstreet Hound Dogs were on the music scene. Zara had convinced herself that she was their biggest fan and was positive that she remembered them when they first started.

As Pippin started the opening verse, the girls began to scream, partly because it was Pippin and partly because they had never seen Pippin with a couple of plums tied to his tail.

Owning the stage, Pippin strutted around carrying off the moves that Eugeen had taught him while singing the lyrics to 'Bones bigger than Life'. Doing the typical boy band thing, Pippin crouched down and touched all the girls' paws, which sent them wild.

"Oh my God Bronte, that is your brother up there! How hot is he!" Nica fanned herself with her handkerchief.

"Yes, that is my brother" Bronte said proudly, "and what is more, he doesn't have a bad voice either."

"Your turn." Pippin nudged Brutus who was panicking and trying to look at the back of his paws to see his back-up lyrics that Eugeen had told him to sing if he forgot the original ones.

"Oh my days, it's Brutus!" cried Olivia, 'He is such a spunk and look at those testicles.'

"Are they meant to be that colour?" Zara frowned; she had never seen orange coloured ones before.

"It's the big fella!" Carlos shouted, "It's Brutus in da house!" which of course got everyone else cheering and shouting their support for him.

Trying to remember what Eugeen had taught him, Brutus strutted down the stage doing what he hoped was a confident and sexy walk. Really he actually looked as though he had rocks in his pants but in his eyes and in the eyes of every dog at the venue, he looked awesome.

Whatever Brutus was worried about that day never materialised. While he did forget his lyrics, he did remember to sing 'I love my Mum' and 'Poo on my bum' at the appropriate times and make it look and sound like that was how it meant to be. He was so convincing that the audience were even singing it as well.

His 'dancing' may not have been perfect, but he did manage to spin around the stage on his back kicking his long brown legs into the air while the other dogs worked the crowd and the audience applauded them.

Chewy played the drums while shaking his long fur like a rock star and doing a bit of head banging. Georgina broke her promise of not being a groupie and removed her leather collar and threw it at Chewie, which hit him on the head and nearly knocked him off his seat.

Fat Harry who can't dance very well, did his best with the backing singing and dancing. The girls didn't notice that he couldn't dance and got out of breath with each movement. What they did notice was how confident and happy he was and that was more than enough for them.

But thank goodness they hadn't noticed that he had lost one of his tangerines and was bouncing about with one orange in his netting bag. God only knows where that tangerine had ended up.

Rocco was singing and replacing the real words with swear words, he did say the word 'bollocks' a lot but he carried it off beautifully and even his invisible friends egged him on.

Kaya's lips had migrated up his teeth but he still managed to play the harmonica and throw in some dance moves as well. This impressed Nica but being much older than Kaya, she had to remind herself of her age and respectability and how finding such a young dog so attractive could be seen as being a 'cougar'.

Rocky had been patiently waiting for his turn and as Eugeen gave him the signal he performed his long awaited wheelie spin that Eugeen had spent so long teaching him to do.

He had one of those small keyboards secured to a strap around his neck carefully placed on his lap so he could play the keyboard with one paw and the other paw resting on his leg.

Rocky had completely forgotten his lyrics and didn't have anything written on his paw to back him up so he made up his own up instead. The audience seemed completely enchanted with the handsome black kelpie singing and playing the keyboard with one paw and doing the odd wheelie on stage.

One Iggy admired him more than any of the others and that was Bronte. Unable to contain herself anymore, she ripped off her collar and threw it at Rocky where it landed smartly on his lap. Rocky initially wondered what it was as girls had never thrown their collars at him before, so it took him by surprise but once he realised who it was from, he gave her a cheeky wink.

Eugeen thought that Rocky fitted the 'Geek Chic' style quite well and doing quirky things with a keyboard and a wheelchair could give the Breeder Boyz the edge over the other canine boy bands.

He never saw Rocky's imperfections and neither did the audience. All they saw were seven dogs having the time of their lives and totally winging it as pop stars. Because they were having so much fun and had stepped out of their comfort zones, there was no such thing as failure.

After the first song

The boys had finished their first song and were slurping down some water. Brutus wiped his sweaty forehead on a towel and then threw it to the girls, and in response they were screaming for a selfie.

Deejay and Carlos were talking to all the neutered boys about the possibility of oranges as testicle replacements. They felt that the idea could really take off until they were reminded about Fat Harry's tangerine, which was still missing.

Pippin's plums were squashed and mushy, but that didn't seem to bother him. Picking up his microphone a breathless Pippin stared at the crowd and waited for them to look up at him.

"Quick! Pippin is going to speak!" Zara jabbed Olivia in the ribs. Olivia didn't reply because she was busy wondering why Pippin had scorch marks on his eyebrows.

"And this is our final song of the evening and is dedicated to everyone that believes in it. Because we all need a bit of magic in our lives don't you think?" Pippin gripped the microphone and gave a little wave to the crowd.

"Pippin we love you!" Zara and Olivia waved scarves at him and were delighted when Pippin waved back.

"Oh my god, I think I am in love." Olivia swooned and fanned herself with her paws,

"Catch me, someone, before I faint" Zara checked to see if there were enough people to catch her should she collapse. Realising that there weren't, she frowned and made a miraculous recovery.

"We love you Brutus!" Madame Gigi called up at him. Brutus winked at her and wagged his tail so hard that it nearly knocked Kaya off the stage.

The boys sing their second song 'Could it be Magic' sung by the fictitious boy band 'Dogs on Point'

As the music started, the boys started to dance; Rocky was playing the keyboard and dancing in his wheelchair as much as his hips would allow him to.

Pippin started to sing, Brutus started to dance (well, more like lying on his back kicking his legs), Fat Harry did a cute wriggle of his butt that caused his other orange go flying and smack Vader the boxer in the face.

Rocco was hitting the drums with his front legs like angry carrots, wearing his Ray-ban sunnies; he looked the epitome of suave.

Chewy was in a world of his own dancing in circles at the end and admiring his own reflection in a mirror which everyone just thought was part of the act. His fur was sticking out the bottom of his jeans making him look like a yeti.

The dogs were winging it really; nobody knew their words so they made up their own. The dancing left a lot to be desired, as most of the dogs had lost their oranges. Pippin's plums were smashed and he had burnt his eyebrows.

Fat Harry had nothing but his empty testicle bag, which he had filled with a small AFL ball and we all know what shape they are.

As the song ended, the audience clapped while chanting 'Breeder Boyz, Breeder Boyz!' and Eugeen ordered the group to line up on stage and take a bow.

Pippin, Brutus, Chewy, Kaya, Rocco, Fat Harry and Rocky took their places and waved to the audience. "What's Fat Harry doing I wonder?" Carlos asked Deejay.

As Deejay was about to reply, Fat Harry took a leap off the stage and yelled something about 'rock stars and crowd-surfing'. Landing on top of an overweight Schnauzer called Klaus, Fat Harry knocked him out of his seat and onto the floor.

"Ouch, that's gotta hurt!" Deejay winced as he caught sight of the Schnauzer's curly bum swirls wedged between two chairs.

Curly bum swirls are the curly bits on either side of your dog's bum, check it out some time, it's rather cute

At the end of the evening

"Thank you for coming, lovely to see you, darling!" Eugeen said robotically to each dog as it left the venue.

A furious looking Klaus the Schnauzer was wheeled out in Rocky's wheelchair. His front right leg was in a sling; he had a bandage around his head and an eye patch over his right eye.

"Klaus my friend, Sorry about Fat Harry, these pop stars are full of high jinx you know."

Klaus replied to Eugeen in a flurry of German that I have been told translated to 'bastard'.

"German is such a beautiful language, it is the language of the Bratwurst sausage and sauerkraut", Eugeen thought to himself and then set about finding Fat Harry to tell him off him for his crowd surfing.

Bursting through the door of the changing area where the Breeder Boyz were getting changed, Eugeen shouted, "Harry darling! Come out wherever you are, there is a small matter of Klaus the Schnauzer to discuss with you."

It took several minutes to find Fat Harry who was eventually discovered in the food cupboard eating a packet of digestive biscuits, which he tried to deny, but the crumbs on his snout gave him away.

Later that night back at Pippin's house

Every dog had returned back to their respective homes that night as pop stars, each dog having enjoyed a taste of fame and popularity.

Eugeen had made Fat Harry send Klaus the Schnauzer an apology letter in German, although I suspect Klaus wasn't amused when he opened it. Let's just say that Rocco helped him write it and used a German translator and many of the words were rude and may or may not have mentioned the war.

Bronte was curled up in her bed complaining that her paws were hurting from all that dancing, how handsome Rocky looked and how Kaya's teeth were just like a toothpaste advert. Pippin was oblivious to her incessant chatter as he was busy in the kitchen making them both warm milk for bedtime.

"I think the night went very well don't you Pippin?" Bronte yawned, "I am so exhausted."

"Yes, yes I do Bronte, well apart from Fat Harry crowd surfing and hurting Klaus the Schnauzer of course." Pippin cringed as he recalled the whole incident.

"Brutus was such a good boy, I told you that he would be OK didn't I?" Bronte said smugly.

Pippin agreed that Brutus had done very well and Rocky too. They had all excelled themselves, and he was pretty stoked with the whole gang. Even the girls had made excellent groupies, screaming and fainting on Eugeen's signal.

Handing Bronte her mug of hot milk, Pippin curled up beside her ready to settle down for the night.

"Oh I know what I forgot to tell you, some elderly poodle made a big complaint that someone had shit in her handbag." Bronte blew on her cup to cool her drink down before taking a mouthful of her milk, "Can you imagine anyone doing something quite so revolting? Apparently, it was the size of a tree log."

Pippin felt his cheeks burning and prayed that Bronte wouldn't notice the guilt that was written all over his face like the print of a newspaper. "Really? How disgusting." Pippin shook his head and buried his snout in his mug.

"I am not even joking and rumours have it that the poodle wants every dog that was at the concert tonight in a lineup, so she can see which dog could have done such a huge turd."

Then after finishing the last of her drink, Bronte kissed Pippin on the side of his snout, "Anyway, I am off to bed, goodnight Pippin and well done on tonight, you did us all proud."

"Bronte?" Pippin said a few moments later.

"Yes Pippin?"

"About that turd in the handbag......"

The End

Thanks and Acknowledgements

I would like to thank the following people:

Dejana Louise for producing the beautiful artwork for the cover of my book. You have captured my characters perfectly and really helped bring them to life. I am certainly looking forward to getting more artwork done by you in the future.

The members of the Italian Greyhound Club of Western Australia for making Brutus and myself feel so welcome in the group—despite me not having an Iggy of my own. Your dogs have all provided me with inspiration, laughs and precious memories and some wonderful friendships have been made from this.

Denise for letting me use her dogs Pippin and Bronte as muses for my stories. Not to mention the cups of tea, honey cake and the chats in your lovely garden, and for helping me to reboot my imagination when it got too hard for me to write. You have been a huge source of creative inspiration for me, and that means more than you will ever know.

Moira for your endless and unwavering belief and support that I could get this book finished, even when I didn't believe it myself.

Lexie, you introduced me to the world of lure coursing, and Italian Greyhounds and our friendship started from there. Our dogs bonded over some roadside puppy temper tantrums and furious flapping of jowls, so thank you for letting me use Vader as inspiration.

Eve for getting my humour on talking animals and for editing my manuscript in what precious free time that you have. Not to mention understanding me when I describe 'whippet jeans' and 'kelpie spectacles'.

Luke for being my soundboard and 'go-to person', I am looking forward to reading your book, and I am sure it is going to be brilliant.

My husband Ab for putting up with the endless chatter about my characters and not complaining when you find Iggies in the house behaving as though they own it, but most of all, just for accepting my passion for writing and supporting me through this journey.

My lovely Dad who has always believed that I could write this book and has been patiently waiting for it to be published. This book is for you Dad, you are about to get drawn into the world of talking animals, and I hope you like it.

About the Author

Samantha Rose is a freelance writer and blogger. She is the author of the popular blog titled, 'The Pigaloo Diaries' and has a particular interest in writing short stories about talking animals.

In her spare time, she enjoys hanging out with her Italian Greyhound friends, swimming with her dogs, and holding meetings with the local parrots that frequent her garden.

Samantha shares her life with her husband, her two dogs, Rocky and Brutus, and a cat called Kevin who has taken over Gordon the cat who crossed over to Rainbow Bridge on 26th August 2017.

Connect with Samantha Online

Thepigaloodiaries.com
Twitter: @GordonInPerth
Facebook.com/My-Dog-Brutus-429308250490560/
Instagram: @juniparose

33661351R00132

Printed in Great Britain
by Amazon